Saga of the Dead Men Walking
Blindsided

Joshua E. B. Smith

CONTENTS

SAGA OF THE DEAD MEN WALKING
BLINDSIDED

Ah yes, the Hunter's Guild. Always an interesting topic. An organization of state-sponsored assassins, thugs, and thieves. They operate in every Kingdom, every Empire. Rulers and Lords always find a use for their ...unique... set of skills. Some, such as Dawnfire, routinely offer them "Writs of Execution" - death sentences to be carried out with no fear of recrimination from the law of the land. Their numbers are immense, and their coffers are always overflowing with bloody gold.

Yet, they have a use. Unique sets of skills always do. There are those in their ranks that specialize in the slaying of monsters, exterminators – at times, confused with the more noble exorcists. That because they too condemn creatures that should never see the light of day, that they are somehow vaunted champions of the Heavens. That they are somehow one of us, simply by their nature.

This is simply not true. There is nothing priestly about them. Most do best destroying things of flesh and blood. The true beasts of the land, not the unholy from under it. Daemons and the Fallen? No. That is our job. Our calling. Our honor.

But they do such a wonderful job in cleaning up what we leave behind.

~Sir Steelhom
Office of Oversight
New Civa

I. THE SUNCURSED & THE TUNNEL-RAT

Some men live by the sword. There's nothing wrong with that. Bladework is an art that goes back in time to the very first person that ever wielded a stick with a sharpened point. It will continue to be so until the last man draws his last breath. Even then it will last eternal in the hands of the guardians of the Heavens and within the ever-churning fires and chaos of the Abyss. Where there is war, there will forever be swords.

Swords, however, are not the end all and be all. A sword cuts. It doesn't crush. It doesn't push. It doesn't freeze. They don't normally burn on their own. While magic and swords go hand in hand – there are very few that can use both. Fewer still that can wield a magical blade.

You could never throw one and reliably knock a man from a battlement. Your luck on the high seas, if armed solely with a sword, would be dictated by how close your ship was to theirs; and if you weren't moored next to it, your fight wouldn't be at a comfortable range. If your goal was to keep your opponent at a distance, a sword did little to help your options. While a sword could be long, it could never be long enough to safely unseat a rider from the ground.

It was a close weapon. You had to be in reach. Hand to make it a fair fight. That wasn't always ideal. Men fight with honor all the time; and honorable men die all the time. Who are the men that live to fight another day? Men of God go and fight for the honor of their God, for to die in the service of one's God is to achieve true glory.

Not everyone is quite that eager.

Some of them have better things to do.

The huntsman looked downrange of his perch. It was pitch black out; nary a star hung in the sky. A bad night to be alone. A wonderful night to hide in the shadows. The only lights to be seen were from the torches and spells that had the courtyard of Castle Talonbur shining under the cloudy skies. The party was grand. The nobles were delighted. They were all so excited and joyous that the thought of anyone wishing ill was far outside of all of their minds.

Only one person knew about the murderers in their midst.

After all – she had hired the one to dispose of the other.

While Duchess Malindara's grand-daughter celebrated her wedding, he drew an arrow from his quiver and took aim at his prey. There were guards no more than ten yards from him in either direction. None of them had any idea that he was there. From the top of the outer rampart to the courtyard it would be a hard shot under ideal circumstances... being so close yet staying hidden from the guards made it a tad trickier.

There wasn't time for anything more than two shots; one for each name on the list. Another man might have tried poison, or magic, or risk getting close with a dagger. But a dagger wouldn't work for his quarry, and magic would be too flashy to do right. All the poisons he had to use were simply just out of the question for this particular job. A sword? To go in, to cut down everyone? He wasn't being paid to kill the entire party, and he wouldn't have tried to do it on his own even if so.

No. A sword was a poor man's weapon. To him, it took little real skill to use even if it did its dirty job well. You take the sharp bit and you push it into the soft bits. That is all a sword was. A bow, on the other hand? A bow let you bring down man or beast before it even knew you were there. It let you do everything a sword couldn't. He took a deep breath, steadied his aim, and let the first shaft fly through his fingers.

There was yet another advantage of using a bow.

The grand-daughter screamed. A bright red blotch appeared on her wedding dress just below her shoulder. She fell to the ground hard, wailing for help and thrashing as blood coursed down her back and arm. Nobody had any clue where the bolt came from. Only one person wondered if it had been meant for him. Wondered too late, at that.

He smiled as he nocked the second arrow for the next shot. The girl would live but her arm would never be the same. A cleric could salvage it, if they hurried... and if the House healer hadn't been sent off into the countryside hours ago. The Duchess had wanted her to be punished. It was a terminal case of disapproval of the wedding. She wanted her to remember it the rest of her days. She wanted suffering, and it wasn't like the groom would be around long enough to experience it.

The second arrow found its mark dead center and true. His victim gave a silent scream as it pierced his heart and lodged itself halfway through his chest. That other reason, why the bow did so well for him? The groom spun around and burned away in a shower of black ash and burning embers before he even hit the ground. A few bones hit the cobblestone and dissolved to dust on impact.

A wooden shaft through the heart put down vampires with ease.

Stannoth was off the rampart and halfway through the citadel before anyone could figure out where he'd been hiding. Not a torch or a spell-cast light illuminated his path. It would be hours before they figured out the way he had escaped and well into dawn before they would even get halfway down his route. He ran a hand over the metal bar that covered his eyes.

In his line of work there were advantages to being able to see in the dark.

The Golden Empire of Mathiea was surprisingly not of any major importance in the Age of Misfortune. It was a *large* nation, an almost completely unified empire that dwarfed the size of the "mainland" kingdoms of Dawnfire, Civa, and the Missian League. Their only concern was the offshoot nations of J'par and Athiea on the eastern edge of the continent... but that was it. By all thought and definition they were a slumbering giant. Nobody cared to challenge them and nobody cared to anger them.

So, they were largely ignored.

That wasn't to say that they had no hatred of war. (Or that they were being left alone on the "spiritual" front.. demons and their kin don't normally care for borders.) On the contrary. One doesn't build an empire without winning battles. Their soldiers were as fine as any other, and mercenaries were one of their chief exports. They just simply didn't have any desire for any more acts of conquest. On a global scale they

3

were a well-bred bitch amongst hungry and vicious rats.

A well-bred *rich* bitch.

Mathiea had won the right to not give a damn. Once they conquered the majority of their own (figurative) demons they decided that gold ran thicker than blood. Merchants whom had already managed to make a nice name for themselves within their borders looked outwards. While other nations saw fit to take new territory by might, Mathiea realized it was easier just to buy it. Less of a fuss, usually. To that end, the Blackstone Trading Company was borne through the efforts of the Emperor and all of his (not entirely) merry men.

While the Golden Empire may have been seen as as sleeping giant, Blackstone was not. The B.S.T. (or the BeaST, as some called it) was as ruthless with coin as an assassin was with steel. Gold was not just a weapon in their toy chest. It was their *favorite* weapon. Everyone and everything had a price and the Company knew it. Even the people who could not be bought always had at least one thing that could be. If they didn't value their own lives, it was a given that someone else could put a price on it. In a quarter-millennium they had never found a person without a price.

Nor did they intend to start now.

It should go without saying then that the BeaST was a heavy investor in all things mercenary — starting with the Guild they themselves founded. The entirety of the Hunter's Guild was built out of the simple premise that life has a price. When gold wasn't enough to solve a dispute, sharpened edges usually did. Business was so good in Matheia that the Guild branched out to the north in the form of a pair of smaller-yet-competing Guilds that grew in the lands of Civa and Dawnfire.

After the Crusades, a branch even formed in the sands of Sycio to the west. That one was doing quite well... the revenge markets always did. The Eastern Kingdoms weren't so welcoming, but, in time. They would be, in time. The rich pigs that spawned the Guild were patient. Blackstone financed the Guild in almost all matters and manners. No matter where or what else the Guild involved itself in, the BeaST was their omnipresent client.

Some wondered if it wasn't their omniscient client as well.

They weren't that far off.

4

Lady Elanis was only too happy to see her lanky hireling three days after the vampire groom and his far too lively bride had fallen into ashes and misfortune. "Huntsman," she had started with, "your timing is impeccable." Not just too happy. *Far* too happy. It was unnerving.

He dropped to one knee and bowed his head to the Guildmatron. Lady Elanis wasn't just the Contractor Agent of a satellite office. No. Lady Elanis was the actual *Guildmatron* of the Southern Guild. Every Hunter that drew coin on this side of the Ocean of Tears collected their pay at her whim. If the Northern Guilds weren't so temperamental, she would be the de-facto ruler of the entire organization. Yet, you wouldn't know it from her office.

It just wasn't all that grand. Her Manor was an entirely different story but the Lady had always lived a life that focused on the professional side of the job instead of the more opulent. The entire building could have been confused for militia barracks in almost any other urban center in the western world. Simple stone walls in simple square stone rooms that blended together one after the other.

That wasn't to say that there weren't some decorations. The Guild Hall itself had no shortage of paintings, rugs, and fancy furnishings. The occasional mounted head (be it animal or other) gave some level of awe for the casual visitor just for the sake of causing awe. Her office was spartan in comparison, other than the dragon skull that had been hanged on the wall behind her workspace.

Scrolls overflowed their shelves on every wall. Maps hung loosely by a handful of wall sconces (and one had been unceremoniously draped over a dragon rib in the far back). Heaven help the woman if a fire ever sparked into existence somewhere in there.

She always had a look of a harried tavern wench, but looks could be deceiving. Disheveled blonde hair, soft skin, lightly tinted blue eyes, and loose clothing would make you think that she was just a maid. You wouldn't think that this small, innocent-looking, unassuming, bubbly woman had personally ordered the deaths of hundreds.

Deaths issued by contract after contract. Writs both small and large for things both living and dead. Monsters and merchants. Abominations and royals. Soldiers and thugs. Taxmen and priests. It mattered little. She wielded the power of the sword through the power of the pen.

Elanis also hadn't let him stand up yet.

It was hard to tell which matron you were going to get any given day. Professional Elanis was a delight when there was a job to be done (and there were always jobs to be done). Perky Elanis was scary, because it meant that she had found something to entertain herself with. Loving and kind Elanis was something he hadn't seen yet. That probably didn't bode well.

She had slid her hand under his hood, her fingernails stroking his visor the moment that he was within range. She was also surprisingly quick. "Stannoth Shi'amar, Huntsman of the Southern Guild. You've been doing us proud lately. And your people... you do your fellow damians a true honor with your acts."

"Thank you, Lady. Glory of the hunt."

"Don't kid yourself. For the glory of the coin."

He had to fight really hard to keep the smirk off of his lips. "Yes."

"You've been with us for... how many years now?"

"Five."

Elanis gave a slight little nod. "You've been with us more or less since you left the Undertunnels, right?"

There was no clue where exactly it was she was going with this. "Yes, Lady."

"And you never care to see the inside of a cave again, true?"

"Yes."

"You are a man of few words. I do admire that of you," she remarked with a soft smile before her voice crumbled just a little. "You know that I would never place one of my boys in a place where it would cause them undue harm in simple pursuit of coin."

"Yes..."

"Coin is the beginning and the end but it's cheaper to use the right tools than break the wrong ones time and time again. Do we still... see... together?"

No reason to mince words even if there was a cold feeling settling in his chest. "Yes..."

She hooked her finger in his hood and drew him up off of his knees. "Then understand the gravity of the situation. This isn't a job with coin as the only goal. I have a writ with your name signed to it. You were asked for specifically."

"Lady...?"

She waved someone out of a smaller waiting room to the side. "Stannoth, allow me to introduce you to Maester Talonbur. You crippled his grand-daughter a few days ago."

Never a good sign. He'd be lying if he said he didn't look for weapons on the older man right away. He was dressed as most merchants of wealth do: gaudily. He wore red and green silks covered with loosely hanging bracelets and earrings dangling over every inch of him. Gaudy, ugly, expensive, and impractical. It wouldn't even have looked good with a hat, which, thankfully, the Maester had decided to leave at home. From the look of it, he'd left his weapons there too. He didn't think that Elanis would sell him out to a vengeful client. It wasn't in her nature.

The elder reached out and clasped one of Stannoth's hands and squeezed it tightly. "Huntsman. It is a pleasure. Please, do not be alarmed. No harm will come to you from me. Business is simply business."

The damian bowed his head. "Yes. Simply business. You understand. Thank you."

"You may not want to do that," he responded.

"Maester?"

"Don't thank me," he cautioned. "While I bear you no ill will, my grand-daughter surely does. She already hired thugs to kill my wife over that bit of business. Once she discovers that the woman is no longer of this world, I fully expect her to send them after you."

Stannoth would have blinked if he could have. "Assassins." He looked over at the Lady. "Sanctioned?"

"No, not sanctioned. I would never," she answered, shaking her head to emphasize it. "It seems I may have put you in a bit of a bind," Elanis began, "but it's a happy accident... in a way. Kind of a happy one. Not... entirely, but... it's kind of one."

"Yes, an accident," Talonbur sighed. "You issued a writ based off of information from my wife to kill my grand-daughter's husband and maim her for life. Now I need a new wife, and the heiress of my fortune needs a new groom."

"Your wife? Not my kill," he contested.

The Maester flicked his hand divisively. "Oh I know. I did." When Stannoth's jaw clenched, the elder shrugged. "I love my grand-daughter." He said it in a way that made it sound like everything was completely normal.

"Unfortunately the groom was also loved. If the Duchess hadn't

7

passed on..." Elanis started.

"She'd suffer worse."

"Yes. Yes, she would have. And now it is safe to say that your life is also forfeit everywhere in this Godling-forsaken land, Stannoth. I wouldn't mind so much either way, because let's be honest, you wouldn't be the first assassin that other assassins wish to claim. As it would turn out, this is a bit of most fortunate timing. You know what they say: success is equal parts talent and candlemarks."

The damian looked them back and forth. The confusion wasn't exactly abated yet. "Deathmark. Not fortunate." He wavered for a moment, then asked the next, most important question. "Good timing, how?"

"Maybe not for the long term," Elanis sighed. "I've always enjoyed your company, Shi'amar. Truly absolutely adore your skills with a bow. I don't want to see you in the ground even if others do. That leaves me without much of a choice."

"The Guild is safe."

"Yes. And I'm sending you to one... a bit safer. Hopefully." She flicked her wrist and a scroll was in her hands. He *watched* her do it. Her hands were empty, then they weren't. The woman was legendary with her ability to make writs out of thin air. He finally knew it. She *actually* could make them just like that. She was magical; a scribe's wet dream. "I've arranged for your personal contract to be transferred to the Northern Guilds. I told Lord Skyan and Lord Draen to fight over you."

He straightened up blindingly fast. "Releasing me?"

She sighed. "Reassigning. But not by choice. You have been requested... and I am sorry, but the request is from the Master. By name."

Not only did he straighten up - he froze. "The Master?"

"Yes."

"Whose Master?"

"The only one that matters," Talonbur answered. "Master Aidenchal."

The name hung in the air. Master Aidenchal. The patriarch of Blackstone. There was no reason that Stannoth could name for the Master to even know who he was, let alone to request his services. Let alone by name. *Any* name.

"Oh, please, pick up your tongue, boy," the Maester sighed. "Were I

8

to have my way, I would pay for thugs to shatter your arms into little slivers of bone and have your fingers fed to pigs."

Elanis flicked a look at the merchant. It was not a warm look. "They would then answer to me. Do not mistake my willingness to forfeit his contract as willingness to forfeit his life."

"Your willingness is dictated by the Master. Nothing more, nothing less."

"Care to place gold on that? We could find out. There are others, were he to disappear."

Stannoth cleared his throat. "Lady."

She didn't take her withering gaze off of the merchant lord. "Hunter, this is a Writ of Investigation and Execution. You won't like where I'm sending you. Again, I'm sorry. You won't be sent alone, for what it's worth."

He opened the scroll and tried for all he could to understand why she would do this to him. "A punishment."

"No, but I can see how you could think that it is," Elanis sighed. He could see the shift in her aura as the irritation with Talonburn turned to sadness over his assignment. "The Kepershal Gem Warren has been the target of a murderous campaign being carried out by person or persons unknown. We have a deeply vested interest in making sure that outpost isn't destroyed."

The damian looked at him again. Just looked. "Dwarves. Sending me... to dwarves. What interest? They're *dwarves*. Not worth interest."

"An interest which is none of your concern," Talonbur interrupted. "Suffice it to say that the interest is there. Transportation arrangements have already been made. You and the other contractor will be departing within the next three hours."

"Lady Elanis, please."

She shook her head. "No. Your life is forfeit if you stay here. If not by the Maester's kin then because of the Master's *disapproval*. My protection can only be used for so much for so long. Neither of us have a choice if you want to stay alive."

It was hard to read a damian's face. The entire race had been cursed to die should they ever see the sun. Not just one of them. All of them. Every single damian that walked the land had daylight stolen from them upon pain of agonizing death. Magic let them see in the dark. But to keep their lives safe? Those that dared to risk leaving their home in the tunnels had to suffer first.

They suffered the feeling of boiling silver and lead poured over their eyes. Stannoth was no different. The lead was enchanted, true, but the pain... the pain did something to them. Not all of them survived it. The magic let them see this world and the magic around all things, and everyone. It let them read a man as easily as a book.

It also made them next to impossible to be read by someone else. To this day, Elanis had no idea if he was angry with her at that moment, or if he merely hated Talonbur. "Yes, Lady."

Maester Talonbur finally smiled. "Good. Now that the pleasantries are over, let's collect your partner. From the sound of things, I believe you two will get along just fine."

A short time later, Stannoth decided that Talonbur was not just an ass.

He was a liar, too.

Goldenglass was an interesting city. An amalgamation of merchants and mercenaries, it took root in a marshland near the middle of Mathiea. To the untrained eye there was no rational explanation for building in such a wet, humid, miserable location. In fact, it went against just about any and all measure of common sense.

But if you ever visited, you'd notice that there were only three roads leading into it. You'd notice that the roads went over bridges or under tunnels, and below those bridges (or over those tunnels) there was water. Now cities with moats were nothing new. A time honored tradition, really, even if it forced the city to build up instead of out. What made this different was that this water didn't have sharks or alligators. Or any fish at all.

No. The moat below Goldenglass was polluted with some of the most caustic fluid known to man. What made it so was a secret lost to time and the mind of the alchemist that had thought it up. It might not have been lost if he hadn't fallen into it immediately after pouring in the last of the solution, but, he did, and it was.

You'd also realize that the "unfinished" walls that stood around the edge of the moat and at various oddly spaced intersections in the city only had holes where the Glassworkers had wanted them. That is to say, where the marshpits were. And the quicksand.

Quicksand, as you could imagine, was a *joy* for the marshes. Why waste walls when you could watch those that meant ill for you and yours to drown in sand? For that matter, the Glassworkers were known for all kinds of *inventive* methods to dispose of threats to the city. They didn't look like much. They didn't *sound* like much. Glassworkers? Men you'd expect to see next to a furnace or polishing a wine bottle. Not guarding a city. They barely had a uniform. Some carried pikes, others swords. Armor was not a major concern. Most of them wore tunics or leather smithing aprons. Some didn't even bother with that much and opted to go shirtless.

Yes, they were undisciplined. Yes, their name was misleading. Yes, they were bullies. However. Goldenglass called itself home to three mercenary groups: Astan's Irregulars, the Drakeforged, and the Hunter's Guild. Nobody had even considered laying siege to the city in a century and a half. It was highly unlikely that would ever change.

Even with the largest vault that the Blackstone Trading Company owned in all of Western Matheia, absolutely nobody thought it would be worth the risk. The BST was everywhere on the continent, and they had their hands damn near everywhere else. It wasn't uncommon to see new faces in and out of the Vault every day (or hour) any more than it was uncommon to see new arrivals marvel at the three towers that made up the Outer Vault.

They were golden, and their upper floors were made out of thick glass blocks.

It wasn't hard to see where the city had gotten its' name.

It was also unlike anything that the other contractor had ever seen. Of course, to be fair, none of the lifelong peasants in the city had seen someone like him either... ever. While he was awed over the towers, children, maidens, soldiers, and whores were all awed over him. It didn't bug him as much as it use to. His people didn't go outside much these days; although most of them just liked it that way. It made him feel somewhat special. He knew he was special, on top of it. He could claim that. He had done a lot, and his people had done a lot.

There was a lot to be said for being a dwarf.

Ever since the cataclysm that had forced his people underground, dwarves – as a whole – had no love for the Kingdoms of Men. When fire rained down and the rocks melted, no Kingdom offered aid. When the Orathalium Empire raided their homes, men watched on bemusedly. When the orcs lost their own lands and invaded the tunnels, their camps full of disaster-weary refugees, men did nothing to aid the Crystal Kingdoms. After the dwarves prevailed, did men offer help to them to rebuild?

No. Men only took. The only race of man that came to their aid were the damians; and even then, the little ones knew it was because they had suffered worse through the way they lost the sun. They had formed an alliance, for a time. It was shaky, but it was an alliance. The races were far more historically friendly with each other than with anyone else.

It should be noted that that didn't say much for their other alliances.

Only, there were two small problems. Neither hunter wanted to see a cave again. That was unfortunate but everybody had a price. The Blackstone had also ignored the fact that while long-term history showed that the damians and the dwarves had had pleasant ties...

...more recent events made just about everyone involved wonder what, exactly, Master Aidenchal was thinking. "An ye bring in th' other hunter. Ye would bring around one of those blind fiskers, wouldn't ye?" That was all it took. One glance. One thought. One mouth.

Their partnership was off to a rousing start.

Historically, their races *had* been friendly. *Had*. When their shaky alliance had faltered, words were said. After words were said, actions were taken. Actions quickly devolved into a race-war. Nobody in the overrealms tried to intervene; they didn't care. While the two sides eventually came to a truce, things between their peoples had not improved much beyond a cessation of overt hostilities.

Talonbur tried to clamp down on the air of hostility with a cough and smooth platitudes.

It didn't work. "A tunnel-rat," Stannoth snapped. "My partner?"

"Oh, ye think I'm a rat, do ye? Well at least *I* cannae see th' sky. Lord Merchant, I know I've already told ye that I dunna need a second body 'n all. That ain't changed any. Fact is, yer wishes an' mine dunna need another body, no matter th' task."

"Now now gentlemen. No need for hostility."

"There is," Stannoth grunted.

The dwarf agreed. "Ye'd best count yerself lucky, boy. See all these weapon-weieldin' fiskers standing here? That's th' only thin' savin' ye from me cuttin' yer stomach out and feedin' yer bowels tae th' dogs."

"Try. Please."

"Lord Merchant, I ain't workin' fer ye if it's with 'im. I just ain't."

With a pained sigh, the Maester snapped his fingers. Those very same men with pointy sticks on their hips drew their weapons. They were a little surprised that the dwarf had noticed them. Nobody else ever really did, so why would these two? Their lack of surprise nearly cost them their lives.

No. If the guards had been trying to surprise them, they failed. Completely.

They moved faster than Talonbur thought to give them credit. The sound of steel sliding out of leather scabbards was matched by the sudden appearance of Stannoth's arrows and Elrok's sword of choice. The damian's arrow was pressed against the temple of the guard to the right of him; his apparent partner-to-be had some kind of hooked blade against the knee of the other. If it was going to end up as a fight, those two guards were going to lose the game long before it could be played. The merchantman cleared his throat a second time. "Your insubordination won't be tolerated either. The two of you have a role to play. A job. You will either perform it and get paid, or I will have you both cut from ear to ear and thrown into the moat."

Elrok raised an eyebrow at his reluctant companion. "I lost me sis in th' Underwar."

"Uncle."

"Ye fight in it?"

"Courier."

"Bodyguard tae th' Underlord."

"Not a good one."

"Th' second one."

"Ah."

Talonbur tried clearing his throat a third time. "While all of this is entertaining, do you two work together, or do I pay the good Lady a fair price for your skins?"

Stannoth looked at the dwarf. The dwarf made an unpleasant sound from someplace lower than his throat. "Ye told me that ye'd explain th' job once th' other Hunter was 'ere."

13

The Maester gestured at the weapons that everyone had out and with a great deal of reluctance, they all lowered them. "I don't know who or what it is that's causing the deaths. We have had other contractors explore various possibilities. No poisons, no gasses. No evidence of disease. Nor is whatever killing them *picky*. The tunnels are ripe with dead burrowers and even a few trolls, so I hear."

"Rats and trolls. Then larger rats," Stannoth interjected, with no shortage of snark.

The look that Talonbur gave him was matched only by the one that Elrok did. "We found the remains of a damian as well."

"Tunnel rats an' then sunblind twats," the dwarf said with a smirk. "An' now tell me how many of me kin have gone off tae th' next life? Four? Five?"

With a shake of his head, Talonbur gave an unpleasant answer. "At least twenty-six. And several contractors."

Elrok didn't take the news well. But he did take it quietly. "Twenty..."

"Six, dwarf. Twenty-six. Oh, and four... let's call them independent contractors. There was a fifth that we had hired. She's gone missing, I've been told."

"Not all hunters?" Stannoth asked. They entered an enclosed courtyard that could have easily been described as a garden sanctuary. Few words were strong enough to describe it or to do it much justice. 'Green,' 'lush,' 'white marble,' and 'far too excessive' would all have to do.

Nobody was paying any attention to it anyways. They were approaching a man in a brilliant blue robe with a golden trim around the hem. A Granalchi Adept; wizards of impressive skill. His presence here likely meant that they weren't going to the undertunnels by way of ship. Teleportation was now on the menu for this trip.

"Two Granalchi, two huntsmen. The fifth that we hired was a freelance murderess... the Master apparently felt that she might have been some use. I'm told she was a dreadful woman. All claws, no class."

"At least thirty bodies? An' yer bringin' in more Hunters when a pair o' us are already dead an' buried? Why not call fer a Holy bastard or two?"

"I attempted to get him to consider the option. He said the last one we employed hasn't quite..."

14

"Survived th' Master's job?" It could have come from either of them. Elrok took the honor.

"...impressed." He wavered a minute. "Master Aidenchal has taken a shine to him for one reason or another, however. If he wasn't so busy... But. We do not feel that this is a matter for a priest. It is a monster of some kind, yet there is no evidence of Abyssian machinations in the caves. What *kind* of monster it is, is for you to discover. Then kill."

Stannoth looked *at* the Maester. He saw more in him than the dwarf could, but he wasn't quite ready to share how much just yet. Even still, one thing was readily apparent. "So we're next. Who after us?"

The man had absolutely no faith that they would survive it. The asshole even hoped they wouldn't. "Ideally nobody," he lied. He handed the blue-robed Adept a purse laden with coins. "We don't want to send anyone else down there we don't have to. The situation needs to be resolved quickly and efficiently. There cannot be any more delays with Aidenchal's plans. So now we have a damian to *see* whatever it is causing the deaths... and a dwarf to track it through the tunnels."

It was Elrok that swallowed his pride first. "Yer kin an' mine dunna work so well together...."

"Too many dead."

"Aye. Tae many tae ignore, or tae put th' thought o' th' old war in th' way over it. Thirty's a damned impressive number. Damned impressive, iffin' nae ghoulish. Care tae see what kinda beastie is bein' such a pain?"

The taller of the two looked over at Talonbur. "The pay?"

"One hundred fifty gold. We do not need the body whole, but we do need proof of execution. If you can make use of anything it has after you cull it, please, do so. I hear your type likes to loot the dead," he added, giving Stannoth a nasty little smirk.

"Lot of coin," he answered, looking down at the dwarf to read his aura.

"Aye, is," Elrok agreed.

"Guild cut?"

Talonbur shook his head. "To be paid separately. The bounty is yours, in full. One-fifty. Each."

The damian gave another disbelieving look at Talonbur. He wasn't lying about that much, at least. Then without a word, he extended his

15

hand to Elrok. With a silent nod, the dwarf clasped it with a heavy shake. It was all the Maester could do to keep from rolling his eyes at the display. He would have lead with the gold if he had thought it was going to be that simple.

Everyone always has a price.

A little bit of fussing later and the Granalchi prepared the spell that would send the pair on their way. It was more or less fortunate for all involved that this was the last time either Hunter saw Talonbur alive. Only one of them would ever come back to Goldenglass – and that was not destined to be at any time soon.

Thank the Gods for such small blessings.

II. THE GEMWARRENS

You could say a lot about the Granalchi. You could say that they were pompous, arrogant, and self-absorbed. You could say that they acted as if they were better than anyone else. You could say that they *believed* that they were better than anyone else. There were good reasons for that.

Mostly, it was because it wasn't just a belief. They actually knew they were.

For one, they were powerful. For two, only the most willful made it through the Academy. For three, they were the very walking definition of 'a particular set of skills.' They had schools that were dedicated to war-magics and nation-building. There were schools dedicated to creating new life and animating the inanimate. There were even schools dedicated to raising the dead and summoning the damned (although the Academy denied that accusation vehemently.)

There were also schools dedicated to helping people at large. For a price, yes, but to help the world. One of their more noteworthy accomplishments was the ability to transport people and things across the continents with the right use of temporal folds and massive amounts of power. Coupled with mass amounts of gold, of course. They didn't work out of the goodness of their hearts. So, for all you could say about them, you could also say that they had wonderful aim.

The portal closed as quickly as it appeared – that is to say, slowly. The swirling blue bubble faded around them with little arcs of lightning scorching the grass at their feet. What wasn't said about their aim was that while it was perfect there were always issues for the passengers over and above the obvious if nobody bothered to say where the portal was sending them.

Winter air hit them and stole their breath away. It didn't steal their shocked curses or settle the transport induced queasiness, but it did steal their breath. It left them both so disoriented, anyone who might have wanted to hurt them could have done so. Easily. It was a thought that neither of them enjoyed entertaining.

Instead of a tunnel or cave, they actually ended up in a small grove next to a rock quarry. A quick glance revealed that humans and dwarves were working side by side. In a way it made sense; if you were a dwarf that had been displaced from your home in the underground, where would you go if given the choice (aside from a comfortable tropical beach away from all threats, foreign or domestic)?

Their stay there was brief. The Foreman – a man by the name of Alanis Yetterdam – didn't tell them much more than they had already gathered. The dwarves in his camp had left the tunnels after the deaths began to skyrocket. They were refugees in all senses of the word. Afraid to go home but unwilling to go far, they had established contact with the overlanders and had bartered a safe haven for as many that were willing to stay.

Yetterdam confided in them that he almost wished that they could stay forever. They refused to just be huddled and hidden from prying eyes. No, they wouldn't take their hospitality without earning their keep, and they were masters at mining and masonry. Production was up, and they were very gracious guests.

Elrok was delighted to hear that his kin were impressing their hosts. Stannoth was just happy that they had left the tunnels. He even openly voiced his hope that word would reach the other warrens that the humans appreciated their skills. Maybe more of them would leave the caves and everyone would be better off.

The overseer didn't understand the depths of his meaning. Elrok did and the remarks didn't earn the damian any positive credit on his account. There really wasn't any pleasing the short little bastard, the other huntsman glumly decided. That, at least, he had the wherewithal not to say out-loud.

Nor did the refugees have much information to offer either. They were only able to really parrot what Talonbur had already said: many

18

dead, no wounded, no idea why. The only people that seemed to have any clue as to what might be going on were the dwarves that had elected to stay down inside the warren itself. Even the healers didn't have a lot to give them to go by. "It ain't a disease," they had offered. "Nae sign o' any kinda sickness nor a damned mark upon 'em. They just died 'n all, nae way tae say what, nae confidence tae rule out th' mundane or th' magical."

In other words: they were absolutely of no help whatsoever.

Alanis was able to answer one question that the two of them had. While they had been told that the problem was in the tunnels in and around Kepershal, their client hadn't given them much information about what was *over* the tunnels of the outpost. He had mentioned it was to the North and was near some disputed territory between the Civan Empire and the Kingdom of Dawnfire. Their assumption that it had to have been part of the borderlands on one side of the feuding nations or the other was just an assumption, but neither of them had ever been so far to the North to really have much experience with the local politics or borders.

The overseer was kind enough to fill them in; they weren't inside the borders of either territory, but instead, in the Equallin Mountains. He called it the "Midland Wastes," which was a more cheerful way of saying "the tunnels are under a depressing scrubland mainly known for rocky peaks, snow, ice, and wandering tribes of bloodthirsty tribal Warlords with no taste for anything but blood and violent sex."

He had actually been less polite than even that. The gist of the response was more important than the actual phrasing of it. Stannoth had a nagging feeling that the region was somehow important... he just couldn't remember why. He eventually just attributed it to some old story or myth he had been told growing up, and he almost let it go, but... He finally put it down in his personal journal while his partner talked to the refugee's leader to figure out how they were going to leave the quarry and get into the tunnels themselves.

As it turned out, it wasn't that difficult of a proposition. While they were capable of it, the dwarves hadn't wasted time by digging their way out. Not when they had their own answer to the magics that the Granalchi used. Why spend the effort to tunnel through rock when you could simply move someone through it with a wave of their hand?

It wasn't exactly a proposition that Stannoth enjoyed. Even still, the magics of a Geomancer weren't to be trifled with (his people had learned that lesson many times over). And that magic *did* work. Even faster than what the Granalchi did.

Only... nowhere near as pleasant.

After the Underwars, the Darkfather and everyone who survived the war knew one thing for certain: the Crystal Kingdoms had their own way of fighting. They knew how to work the bones of the world as deftly as any necromancer could work the bones of a man. They just had so much more to work with. Conventional warfare was not something they bothered with. It was a painfully taught lesson for the sun-blind. The orcs learned it before them. The goblins before that.

They all fought and they all lost. There was a reason why the Kingdoms of Man didn't try to spread below. They were lucky that the dwarves didn't care about the Overrealms... if they had, many of those that knew their history knew that it would truly be hard for the Kingdoms of Men to win.

But what made them so deadly? Was it their skills with blades? Their power with magic that gave them dominion over all things rock, stone, dirt, and gem? Could it have been their willingness to strike from underfoot? Was it that their women were hardier than most men? Or maybe that they knew the monsters that lived underground, and had no qualms with training them to fight in their stead?

All of those things did. They did, because of one skill the short ones had mastered: misdirection.

If Kepershal had been an outpost overland, it would have looked exactly like any other fortress from almost any other fiefdom. Square buildings, thick walls, ramparts carved into the groundstone itself, even iron gates. The dwarves copied all of that. All of it built in caverns with high ceilings and even the occasional moat. It was all there, down to the last grayish brick. The trap was sprung once the victims walked inside any of those "normal" buildings.

Hallways turned to mazes, chambers were built to cause cave-ins. Every twist and turn was full of false walls, pit-traps, and statues crafted of living stone. Of course, if you survived those, you would still have to survive the aforementioned monsters, weapons, and (their) women. Their defenses were something that they prided themselves on (as well they should).

So the discovery that there was a 'dead' human in one of those pits wasn't a huge surprise. The fact that it *wasn't* dead was a bit more of a concern for all parties involved. The creature was still clawing at the pit it had been thrown into, which was impressive, considering the shape it was in. For lack of better words or understanding it was a mass of skin and bone, shredded, ripped apart, yet somehow still standing – and even fighting to get free.

A stone spike jutted through an armpit and out the opposite shoulder. Its throat had a gash that eagerly bled everywhere. He hobbled on a twisted leg. His chest was covered in scratches. Half of its left hand was missing. The fingers on his right hand were worn down to bloody bits of bone from the effort it was putting forth to get out of the trap.

The first thought was that it was some kind of twisted undead monstrosity. Somehow it wasn't. The three dwarves that had delivered the huntsmen to it couldn't understand that it wasn't. They didn't believe it. Their own clerics had said it wasn't, but that wasn't possible. It reeked of death. It *could not* have been alive.

One look from Stannoth and the answer was simple. Impossible, but simple. "Alive."

"Nae. There is nae way that *thin'* is still breathin'."

The taller hunter even tapped his visor like he thought it would change things. It didn't. He couldn't believe it either. "Not dead. Not animated. Just not dead."

"Ye sure yer face ain't broken? That it ain't castin' some kinda enchantment on ye?"

"You love your sons."

"An' me daughter," Elrok added before he realized what he had said. He looked at the archer with a slow look of anger growing in his eyes. "Never said I've ever had any lil'er ones. Know I didn't tell ye that at all."

"Aura did. Can see you clearly. That? It's not dead. Harder to see. But not dead." The damian shrugged again. "Just... is. Don't know what. Just is."

The damians had their own advantages in the Underwars. Not as many, but they had them. "So iffin' 'e ain't dead, what is 'e? Demon-like thin'? Fallen critter from th' Mount?" Elrok looked back down at it and spit. "Some maddened wizard from th' over-realm? Please say wizard. Cannae stand 'em. Me belly is still pissed at th' one that tossed us tae th' quarry."

"No. Not a demon. Not Heavenly. Not... magical. Just old."

"So we cannae kill it, an' it ain't damned an' ain't blessed. What a lovely lil' thin' it is."

"Didn't say we couldn't. Just isn't. Yet."

"Lovely 'n all..." Elrok stared at it and frowned. "Well then. I ain't got any kinda idea floatin' around in me head. Any chance there's somethin' spinnin' around behind that mask o' yers?"

Stannoth looked around at the small crowd (no pun intended) that was gathered around them. "Ask questions. Get answers."

"Yer an annoyin'ly vague man, ye've been told this, aye?"

He ignored it and pointed over his shoulder. "They'll won't tell me. You'll ask instead. You'll get further." The crowd had looked back at him. Nobody was exactly happy to see one of his kind in their midst. A few had even put their hands on the pommels of any weapon they could reach. There was the usual collection of swords and daggers although most of them carried hammers, and maces. All of them looked like they'd be just as happy if he joined the creature in the pit.

"An' that 'e would," a new voice ventured. A dwarf in golden-scale armor with a gnarled stone staff in his hands had pushed his way forward. Like many of the others, he had a long, thick, beard with a round face and coal-colored eyes. Unlike them, he had a bald head with a latticework of scars and... rubies? They were sunk into the skin, and there was more than just red stones.

If the damian could have blinked, he would have. Rubies, chunks of quartz, and emerald fragments had been embedded in his scalp. It wasn't just a fashion statement. A deeper look revealed what he was. *Dwarven magic. Quaint*, he muttered in the back of his mind.

Elrok straightened up. "Gemwarden! Fanim, good tae see ye again."

"Underprince, 'tis an honor."

Stannoth whipped his head to stare at his companion. *That* he hadn't seen. His shock was completely ignored. It was there for anyone to see, but it was completely ignored.

"Nay. I gave up th' title an' all years an' years back."

22

"Dunna change th' man, me friend. Abdication only means ye leave th' Gemset, dunna mean ye still ain't a prince."

This was all news to the damian – but it did serve why Elrok had been picked by name. Royalty does have privileges, after all. Now if only he knew why he had, he'd feel better about all of it. "True enough, I suppose. I'ma sorry tae have tae come this way on such bad business 'n all. Looks like ye've run intae somethin' from a bad vein of rock-luck."

The way that the dwarves had melded their culture so completely with all things in the ground was an oddity even in the wide and varied history of the world. Nobody else had ever even tried to make themselves as one with the land as they did, down to the last title and the last peasant (or as they called themselves, 'pebbles'). Topside, some considered it funny. Most considered it violently annoying.

Stannoth fell firmly on the latter side of that equation.

The Gemwarden cleared his throat. "Worse than bad. What all have ye been told?" After a few minutes of repeating what they had heard elsewhere, Fanim finished while absentmindedly braiding his beard. "Then ye've heard almost everythin'. Th' only other thin' that we know is that whatever this damn thin' is, it ain't natural tae th' tunnels."

"You know how?" Stannoth pressed.

Fanim finally acknowledged his presence with a quick glare. "Th' stone is pained. Iffin' it was a natural critter, th' ground wouldn't be cryin' an' all. Everyplace this *thin'* has wandered tae, th' world has winced under it. It ain't supposed tae be down 'ere. It ain't born 'ere, it ain't bred 'ere, and it ain't right tae be 'ere."

"If it's wrong?"

"Th' groundstone never is." The short huntsman answered. "It's been around longer than th' folk above or below, an' it'll be 'ere everlong after we be gone."

The damian digested it slowly, face even more stoic than usual. When he spoke up again, he changed the topic completely. "One of mine killed. Save the body? Send to a Shadewell?" He held out an outside hope that maybe her body would tell a different story than what the little people had. It wasn't a misguided hope but the name he dropped did *not* go over well with the locals.

A few of the dwarves flinched. The Shadewells weren't friendly places for anyone but the suncursed. Places known to house lost souls; damian men and women afraid to cross over less they run afoul the same creature that had condemned their race in life. They were a place to honor the dead and protect the damned.

They took that protection seriously. Those outsiders who committed crimes against his people were often sent there to suffer for their sins. No. They were not friendly to anyone but those marked and lost to see the light of a mid-day sun. The dwarves knew this. Fanim's response shouldn't have come as a surprise.

"Th' Shadewells? Now why would we be doin' a thin' like that?"

"Sent to the Family?"

That was another title that drew some disgusted looks from the crowd. Fanim smirked at him. "I fear that ye mistake us fer ones that care fer yer customs. Nae, what happened after 'er death ain't a concern o' ours." He watched the mercenary grow coldly furious and kept baiting him on. "An' nae, if ye think we'd just leave a corpse sittin' around doin' nothin' but rottin' away, ye've lost whatever sense ye might've had. I consigned it tae th' stone. Even now, it slides tae Kora's Heart."

Stannoth bristled at the implication. "Entombed him?"

"A 'im? Boy, if ye dunna even know th' difference between a man an' a woman, ye've nae right tae be demandin' answers from us. Sh' was a bit o' a bitch, if ye must know. But nae! We sent 'er off tae th' Heart o' th' World."

"Sent her soul deeper. In the dark," he snarled back.

"I'ma sure it found it's way up an' outta th' tunnels. But it's nae real importance tae us. Ye really think that'd there's a one o' us that'd give a care? Yer as daft as ye are blind."

He may not have liked swords, that was true. That did nothing to stop the huntsman's hand from finding the hilt of the small axe at his waist. He didn't bother with a vocal response. The sheer gall and disrespect shown absolutely offended him to no end.

The only thing that stopped him from re-kindling the war between their peoples in that moment was the hand that quickly tugged at the back of his cloak. Elrok looked to him and mouthed an ineffectively calming word of warning. "Truce, boy, th' truce."

Stannoth grunted in disgust and seriously considered it anyways. "We respected your dead."

"An' that may be th' only reason yer people weren't wiped away in th' war," Fanim continued to taunt.

Quickly interrupting, partly out of fear of rekindling the entire war all over again, Elrok spoke up and scolded the Gemwarden. "Aye, I'ma none tae thrilled either 'n all, Fanim, but we be 'ere tae help. Did ye at least save *any* of th' bodies?"

"Nae. Nae need. Dead be dead; they needed tae be sent on tae th' Heart."

With a glare, Stannoth turned to his otherwise unwilling companion. "No bodies. No evidence."

"Really? Ye didn't save *any* o' 'em?"

"Nae. We looked at 'em an' checked 'em an' sent 'em off tae th' heart, blessins be tae their souls." The Gemwarden was absolutely unapologetic over it. His arrogance was *not* his best feature. It was in a close contest with his bigotry, but it was still barely winning the title as his worst trait.

He was also hiding something. The longer the Hunter glared at the bastard the more he could see something wavering in his aura. Well hidden, way too well hidden, for it to be any good. Sadly... he couldn't tell what. Worse, the longer that the two dwarves talked, the less he trusted his partner.

That wasn't good. "Her gear. Save *it*?" he snapped.

"Stanny, ain't no cause fer anger, dunna ye think ye might be over-reactin'?" Elrok interrupted again in a fruitless attempt at smoothing things over.

"No." A *completely* fruitless attempt. "It's warranted."

Fanim gave him the dirtiest of glares. "Aye. We saved 'er last few possessions. Didn't care tae risk some kindae magic blowin' up in our faces iffin' we missed a trap in 'em. Just waitin' fer all this mess tae wind down befer we pitched 'em intae some pit."

It was the first good news he had heard. "Wise of you."

"M'boy, we ain't accomplishin' a thin' 'ere," Elrok chided with an exasperated sigh. "Fanim, ye have anythin' at all ye can say about this beastie? Th' ground screamin' is a bit of a clue, even if there be nothin' else fer us tae look at. Pretty much rules out disease, tae be sure. Poison an' toxins down 'ere never set well with th' soil. An' rules out anythin' born in th' ground, bad air, dust-worms, things o' that nature. Th' world'd know what they are."

While Stannoth wrestled with the desire to put an arrow in his throat, the Gemwarden gave his companion a nod. "There's been a

25

rumble in th' walls. Been feelin' more an' more bodies bein' sent intae th' ground from up above. An' more than a few be workin' their way back out o' it. Idiot menfolk out there, never gave a damned thought tae what they shove intae th' dirt. Nor th' damned mess they make gettin' outta it."

The dwarven hunter made a disgusted grunt from somewhere past the back of his throat. "Always th' damned dead. Bloody gotta say that this job's taught me that even iffin' I end up in th' pit after me heart stops, be easy enough tae climb outta it. So is it more buggery like th' one at yer feet?"

"Older," Fanim answered. "Some much older than that thin'."

"Old dead. Wonderful," the damian grunted. "What kind?"

"Th' dead kind. Been loathin' it every time th' dirt swells up an' ejects another one from its grip."

"Do ye have any idea what's goin' on up there?" Elrok looked up at Stannoth while rubbing his eyes, hoping he would have figured something out by this point. "Or any idea on th' *type* of dead wakin' back up?"

"Types? A corpse is a corpse. What's th' difference from one drippin' body tae another?"

That made the huntsman unleash a pained sigh. "A great deal."

"Well. Nae that it matters. Nae. I've not a damned clue. But I can tell ye right now, iffin' th' humans are causin' a level o' pain fer each other an' th' results are costin' th' lives o' th' good souls beneath their feet an' all, I'll be personally gettin' what we need tae make damn sure there's *compensation* fer our losses," he promised, arms crossed with a cold smirk.

Struggling to keep the peace and make sense of the mess, Elrok looked down into the pit and shook his head. "So, we've got a thin' there that ain't dead, but should be. Got a pile o' bodies that shouldn't be dead, but are. An' there's dead up walkin' about, summoned by some human or other with issues with th' livin' playin' around under th' damned clouds, jus' tae give us an extra headache."

"Well," Fanim started with a nasty smile, "We were able tae find somethin' that ain't right down 'ere. If ye'd been a few hours later showin' up an' all, we'd have already left goin' fer it."

"For what?" Stannoth asked. He tried looking past the Gemwarden's walls, but didn't quite...

26

He cleared his throat. "I cannae say if yer... special magic... could tell, but I'm all but certain that th' cause is an orc. Some o' th' gate guards caught sight o' it before it went scrambling back intae th' deeper tunnels. I've been preparin' a war party fer it. Maybe th' humans spawned it up, maybe they didn't. Going tae hunt it down an' cut off it's head, an' then we're gonna be findin' out who went an' brought it back tae life."

"First yer blamin' humans, an' now?" The shorter hunter tensed up. "Now, yer blamin' an orc? Ye think one o' those green skinned little shits is behind so many o' our kin gettin' killed? Could ye at *least* make up yer mind befer we run off tae try not tae get killed by th' bastard?"

"It does make sense, dunna ye think? They ain't exactly friendly tae our folks."

"You butchered them," Stannoth pointedly reminded him.

"They wanted our tunnels. They didn't exactly win, now did they? Ye should know all about that. Maybe one o' 'em thought it would try tae get some measure o' revenge fer past wrongs." Fanim was almost... gloating... over it. "I'ma sure that there's nae shortage o' yer folk that'd be interested in doin' one thin' or other that'd have th' same desire tae wipe us out," he taunted, a nasty eye turned to the archer.

Desperate to keep the damian from painting the cave with Fanim's throat, Elrok stepped between them and lifted his hands to hold them both at bay. "I find it hard tae believe that some lowly lil' *tusker* could've called up somethin' like that critter," Elrok said with a measure of bewilderment as he looked back and forth between them. "Could it be a litch, maybe? Those buggers tend tae get all kinds o' bitchy..."

A new voice – a woman's voice – spoke up. "And ye'd be right. 'Tis hard tae believe, cause it ain't."

At the same time, the huntsmen turned to look at the new arrival and her escort. Shorter (and younger) than the other dwarves in the room, this one had an unmistakable aura to her. She radiated leadership, command, and control, all wrapped up in a tiny little package. Stannoth started to warm up to her the moment he saw her, if for nothing else, than out of respect for the aggravated way that half of the other dwarves looked at her. The other half looked absolutely delighted. And then he warmed a little more by the way she looked at *him*. Then he saw the look Fanim gave her.

That look alone just about made him fall in love with her.

27

For a little one she wasn't unattractive. She was still a tunnel-rat, but she wasn't unattractive. Muddy brown hair matched auburn eyes, with freckles that ran across her cheek and down her neck. They stood out in contrast to the rest of her pale skin, and she blushed a little as she watched him try to puzzle her out. "There's been nary a soul that's headed out intae th' caverns that's come back tae us in any other way but dead. Nae orc has that kindae skill, livin' *or* dead. Never befer, never will. I can assure ye o' that."

For a second, there was a flicker of untruth around her. But only for a second. To even suggest that there were orcs around was incredibly odd, let alone the idea that she might have been lying about their presence. The Orathium Empire had been wiped out decades ago, with next-to-no survivors left behind.

Odd, Stannoth mused quietly to himself.

He was the only one to give it any thought, so he let it slide.

"Oh, would ye see some damned reason, ye bloody wench? It cannae be anythin' else," Fanim snapped. "Human scum prolly just raised up some garbage that's pollutin' our homes. Rasin' orcs. Serves 'em right should they get wiped out an' all. An' once again, we gotta clean up th' mess that those bastards started, an' now we're payin' fer it. Gonna make '*em* suffer fer it tae. Ye can watch me; but I'll be makin' 'em pay."

"Ye won't dae anythin' o' th' kind, or th' Underking will make ye drag a coal-cart with yer *personal* set o' pebbles," she snarled before turning back to the huntsmen. "Ye won't find a damned thin' out there, boys. Whatever magic that walkin' corpse is usin' tae stay up an' walkin' ain't nothin' that any tusker tribe has ever gone an' used. Certainly not th' Orathiums – an' they're th' only tribe native anywhere near 'ere. An', frankly, there's barely but a handful o' 'em left, tae boot. They wouldn't risk us commin' fer 'em with a grudge on our backs. Th' humans wouldn't be half that damned stupid either. Never anger th' unders. Even th' mad know that."

Elrok looked at the girl – and she was really just a girl – and frowned. "I know I've never seen ye befer, but I cannae help but think I know ye from a place 'er other."

She flashed him a dazzling smile while Fanim tried to hide his irritation. He failed. "Bayetta! Mind yer place girl; ye've nae say in what these tae get from any o' us," he growled. The damian didn't even bother to hide his delight at his discomfort.

The look she flashed to the Gemwarden had nothing to do with a smile at all. "And iffin' *ye* had done *yer* job, then we'd nae be caught in this damned mess," she argued. "Ye've failed yer charges, an' th' Crown is damn tired of yer excuses. Ye ain't so stupid as tae really think it's *just* an orc."

There was a small grumble of support from the other dwarves present... something that Fanim hadn't had yet. Stannoth wasn't sure that it was such a good thing. It was a start, but she was still a dwarf. That alone made him wonder if the shine he was taking to her was wise or not yet. "Rogue orc. Low threat. Quick kill."

"Aye, it would be. Wish it was," she said with a smile. Fanim tried to interrupt but she would have absolutely none of it. "Hunters. Good tae meet ye both. I'ma th' one that sent fer th' pair o' ye."

"You? Not him?" Stannoth asked, gesturing to the Gemwarden. You didn't have to have magic to see how angry Fanim's aura was turning. The damian really, truly, did not care. A quiet part of him even enjoyed watching it.

"Aye, that I am. I'm sorry we lost th' people befer ye. Sorry about yer girl, tae. Wouldn't have called fer ye if we didn't think it was bad enough tae risk callin' more outsiders tae clean up th' mess. Let alone have tae call on yer guild twice. But, it is, an' I did. Only got 'ere a day an' a half ago meself. Had word sent off tae ye before I left me home. Couldn't trust th' tunnels tae be entirely safe, took th' long way a walk 'ere."

"Didn't need to," he answered. "Others would have come."

"Eventually," Elrok added. "An' ye could've warned *us* not tae go by Geomancer travel. If ye ain't none tae willin', we probably would've gone an' skipped it tae..."

She gave him an odd look. "Ye were tae be told not tae travel down that way... I had heard that th' ground-mage had gone topside, but 'e was tae burrow ye a tunnel down... nae send ye by magic."

"He didn't," Stannoth replied. "Wonder why."

There was a disgusted growl from somewhere in her throat. "We dunna have time tae hate on each other. Fiskin' fools..."

Recognition flashed for the shortest mercenary while he stared at her. "Oh I *dae* know ye! Yer Desavia's daughter!" he all but shouted.

That meant something to someone, Stannoth was sure. Just not him.

"Aye. Th' one an' th' same. I know who ye are tae, ye know." Then she turned and sized up the taller of the pair. "An' I know who ye are. Heard of ye... did some damage out in th' Cursed Wastes o' Agromah, didn't ye? All by yerself, at that?"

"I did. Personal hunt."

Elrok raised an eyebrow. Well, that made things a *lot* more interesting. People didn't go there if they didn't have to. People sure as all the pain in the pits didn't go there on their own. *Th' boy must have some kindae death wish,* he thought to himself. *Just what I needed tae make this trip even better.* "Culled yerself a pair o' litches, aye?"

"One. Other was still mortal. Hadn't changed yet." He paused for a moment and flashed an unwelcoming smile. "He never got to."

"Good. Ye've a talent fer killin' thins that dunna take a blade nae tae easily. Pretty sure we need a bit o' that down 'ere. Question is iffin' yer able tae dae more than jes cut up critters that ain't 'ave a care fer anythin' more than escapin' th' pits. An'... in truth an' all, I needed tae have someone with yer special way of lookin' at things. Truly hope ye didn't mind th' personal invitation."

With her knowing so much about him, he absolutely didn't like knowing nothing about her. It was quickly making him lose some of his stomach for the girl. "Barely know him," he said, pointing down at Elrok. "Don't know you. You sent for us. What are we after?"

She paused and sized him up. Apparently she liked whatever it was she saw. "Aye. I think I got a mind fer what yer victim-tae-be is gonna be, when all's said an' done. What I'ma thinkin' Fanim ain't told ye yet is that that damned thin' down there ain't th' only one an' all, jes th' only one th' hunters were able tae catch. An' none o' 'em got th' smell o' an orc about 'em."

"More?"

"Aye. An' what else 'e ain't told ye yet is that yer girl didn't die th' same day or way that th' other mercs dropped dead an' all from, either. Sh' ain't gone easy, tae... an' down in th' warren proper, deep down in there." She gave a cringe as she remembered something. "Nae. Sh' didn't die easy at all."

"Fanim's convinced."

The other dwarf glared. "How funny, now ye opt tae take me side? Aye, it's th' orc. Gotta be. Ain't nae other cause fer it. That, or it's th' humans. Fer that matter, it could be an orc *sent* by th' humans tae keep us busy."

"Did 'e tell ye about th' journals yer... ye call 'em yer... Night somethin'... whatever 'er title was."

"Nightshade?"

"Aye, that was what sh' called 'erself."

Stannoth tensed up hard. Whatever had killed the other dwarves had taken out a Nightshade? A necromancer. And not *just* a necromancer. A war-trained one. They *only* played to win. At *any* cost They weren't to be trifled with. *Ever.* It was no wonder she died badly – the woman would have ripped open a portal to the Abyss if it meant coming out on top (especially if her life was in immediate danger). He struggled with that earlier urge to pull his axe free. "She had supplies. You stored them."

"Aye, we did," Fanim groused. "But iffin' ye think that yer gonna find a damn thin' in 'em that ye'll be able tae use, yer dead wrong. None o' th' guards that looked at it saw anythin' of note, an' I canna say that even I saw a damned thin' worth makin' a fuss about."

Stannoth shook his head. "You looked. I didn't. You wouldn't."

"Yer still nae gonna find anythin' with their stuff. Yer answers gotta be outside th' outpost walls," the Gemwarden stated matter-of-factly. "Even then, good luck tae ye. Yer chasin' ghosts. Whatever that caused it ain't claimed a soul in nearly three weeks."

"Just means that it's gone an' found other souls tae claim instead o' ours," the girl seethed. "Fer now. What dae ye plan on doin' iffin' it comes back, eh? See which o' yer people gets sent tae an early grave next? Run out an' chase ghosts yerself? That kinda idiocy is why they sent *me* 'ere tae clean up yer mess."

"It means that either th' thin' has moved on or one o' th' hunters or that blind damian bitch managed tae hurt it and scare it off. An' iffin' it didn't, I'ma takin' that tusker's head," Fanim argued.

"Ye dunna 'scare off' somethin' that's eaten this many people!"

Famin stood up to his full (short) height and tried to physically intimidate her. "It's as sure an' obvious that somethin' moved in, an' that orc is th' only thin' it can be! An' after, once it's dead an' all, if fer some reason more o' us keep runnin' intae th' dirt, we close th' warren off, an' we dig out a new one a half-century miles away an' we move on with our lives. May just be that th' tunnels simply ain't safe fer us here nae more. Th' world changes, ye know this, we all dae."

It absolutely didn't work. "Th' tunnels ain't ever safe, Gemwarden, and it's yer job tae keep th' people o' *this* Warren safe. Ye haven't. Ever since th' fall of th' Orathium tribe, this Warren has been damn safe. A pinnacle o' happiness an' joy. An' that's why I've been sent tae 'ere. 'Cause ye've gone and ruined it... ain't safe nae more."

His hands clenched up and he gave her an angry glare. "Ye think that I've got nae control over this. Me governance ain't somethin' even ye cannae question. Ye ain't going tae find a speck o' dust outta place. I dunna care what ye think or yer mother thinks or anyone – anyone else! - goes an' thinks – but until this, this, disaster an' thins, me warren 'as been nothin' but done with rigid perfection. Their answers ain't gonna be in 'ere, an' they're welcome tae come *behind* us when we find an' kill that beast."

"Which? Human? Orc?" Stannoth interrupted.

"Eh. Yer at least right on somethin'," Bayetta challenged, ignoring the damian. "Th' answers tae this curse are damn far out, far as all fisk tae be believed." She turned her gaze over to the two Hunters. "I'll save th' two of ye some time – yer nae gonna find 'em 'ere. But I damn well know that ye won't have tae leave th' comfort o' our lil' home 'ere tae get 'em. I dunna have th' strength or I'd dae it meself."

That's when the damian took a much longer, harder look at the newest arrival. Then he realized two things – and kicked himself, hard, for the second one. Firstly, there was nothing in her aura that didn't like. And he didn't like that. Nobody is ever perfect. Nobody. Most definitely *not* a tunnel-rat. There it was though – a soul that had everything open and everything that he wanted to see.

No, not what he *wanted* to see. What he *needed* to see. What *she* wanted him to see. What she was projecting was that she wasn't trying to blow them off. She really believed that it was more than just some stupid tusker, and she *really* didn't harbor anything remotely resembling an affection towards the Gemwarden. He couldn't tell how much of that was true, and how much wasn't. The moment he realized that she knew what to do to make him believe every word she had to say, any stomach for the woman expired on the spot.

The other? The part that was far, far more problematic?

He couldn't see much past her. His sight, his window into the world between worlds, the one and only advantage he had in these damned tunnels, was muted. It was like trying to see through a fog that had been lowered on him (and just him). That was bad. He didn't have words to describe how bad it was. He had been so busy focusing on what was in front of him that he didn't even notice how badly his sight had been clouded.

"Not here, but here?" Stannoth tried to clarify. *Dwarven double-talk*, he grumbled in his head.

Elrok had been quiet for a while through the exchange. That ended as an idea blossomed hard in his head. "Th' veil. Ye think that our answers an' all can be found in th' ether."

Bayetta gave him a nod. Fanim didn't. "Th' veil ain't a safe thin'. Ye'd be more than better off tryin' tae track where yer other contractors went off tae by goin' intae th' tunnels," he warned.

"Th' veil is th' only thin' that nobody has had th' stomach tae check. Maybe if ye had, then maybe we wouldn't have had tae chip so many names intae th' stone. That's yer only way tae find out th' fate o' these people, an' tae make sure that nobody else follows 'em."

"The veil," the damian stated. She nodded. Before anyone else could say anything else, Stannoth put his hand on Elrok's shoulder and spoke softly. "Talk. Privately. Now." After a glance at his suddenly-stoic expression, the little man agreed. Neither Bayetta or Fanim tried to stop them, but the vibe that the taller hunter was putting off had Elrok utterly worried.

Worried, even, to the point that he didn't put up a foul word for being interrupted once they were well outside of earshot. "Dwarf. Do you trust her? Bayetta?"

He gave a slow nod as an answer. "Aye, I dae."

"Who is she?"

"Why do ye care?"

"Says everything right."

"Sh' says th' truth of th' matter."

"Faking her aura."

"Ye mean it's clean o' deception?" Elrok shook his head, confused. "Ye dunna like 'er, cause sh' be tellin' us th' truth?"

"Everybody lies. "

"Well, Bayetta ain't just anybody." When his partner continued to just stand there, he clarified. "I knew 'er mother. Great lady an' all. Trained all o' th' old Underguard, kept 'em alive in th' worst o' times an'

33

happy an' all in th' best o' times."

"Daughter of a Stonebuilder," Stannoth muttered. "Interesting."

"Nae. Daughter o' *th'* Stonebuilder. Th' one that built th' bridge that ended th' war between our folks. Sh' be a lovely lass. Dunna know what sh's involved in now, but from 'er tone, an' th' way sh's orderin' th' Gemwarden around... gotta be somethin' ranked well and high. An' sh' did call fer us by name, sh' said. But why dae ye worry about 'er?"

"My job. The Gemwarden. You know him."

The dwarf scratched at his chin. "Aye... 'cause 'e an' me brother both served together with 'im in th' wars. Ain't nae shame in that, now is there?"

"Don't like him. He can rot."

"I dunna think ye like many... though, true, ye've got reasons enough."

"No. I don't," Stannoth grunted. "Think he's right. It's an orc," he conceded, odd as it was to even suggest it. "Maybe more. Raid with them. Kill it. We're done."

"Nay. We need tae see in th' ether," Elrok said, disagreeing.

"No. Read Nightshade's journal first. Hunt, kill, after."

"That journal will tell us nae a damn thin'. Ye heard Bayetta, sh' already went an' looked."

Stannoth shook his head. "She did. She's not me. Wants you in ether. Don't trust her." If the defeated damian didn't trust the locals any more than he did... then there was no way that the Gemwarden would have found anything. Neither would anyone else. Unless – or until – the right person could come and find it. It wouldn't be a stretch if she had something special up her sleeve.

"Sh' knows that it may be th' only way tae see th' cause o' what's goin' on..."

"Not safe there. Wait and read."

"Says ye. Ain't yer kin that's gettin' slaughtered an' all. We wait fer ye tae read through a book, an' Fanim's gonna be off tae comb through th' tunnels, an' I'm in nae mood tae see 'im killed, even if 'e is an asshole. Iffin' I tell 'im I'ma gonna scout through, then that might well keep 'im from goin' out an' diggin' around on 'is own."

"Was my kin."

"Just th' one. Nae twenty some odd heads!"

"One too many," the damian snapped. "She's pushing. Could be

34

anywhere. You don't know. Veil *isn't* safe."

"An' Fanim is tryin' tae get us out from underfoot. I know th' bugger. He dunnae lie any tae well, so I can promise ye, 'e's *always* got somethin' cookin' in th' back o' 'is heart."

"Neither have helped. Answer is still hidden." He looked back over his shoulder. "Don't trust either. Going to kill us. Have to think."

Elrok bristled up. "What are ye gripin' over? Th' girl's open, an' ye think that makes 'er some kinda troublemaker o' some kinda... what? An' yer absolutely daft tae be blamin' *'er* when it's even obvious tae *me* that Fanim's got somethin' in 'is pocket!"

That got a small smile from him. "He has power."

"So?"

"Power has secrets."

"An' yer more inclined tae trust th' man that's hidin' secrets than th' one ye can see straight?"

"Yes."

The dwarf didn't quite know what to say to that. So, he didn't. "Whatever went an' gone through this place has aimed tae tear apart or chase off th' people an' things that'd know what tae do about it. True an' all?"

His partner gave him a small nod as a response.

"Was Bayetta tellin' us th' truth that sh' just got 'ere?"

"She was." He wavered for a moment, unsure to tell him about the fog in his sight. "I think."

"Ye think? So much fer that damian special sight," the other remarked with a snarl.

Stannoth let it slide without a response. It *was* a valid critique.

"An' Fanim? Bein' honest about what 'e thinks?"

There was a longer, more uncomfortable pause. "No."

"But 'e is hidin' somethin', ain't 'e?"

"Bigotry," he grunted.

Elrok coughed. "I said 'e's *hidin'* somethin'. Is 'e?"

"Yes."

"Our choices are tae look at th' veil, waste time lookin' at remains o' whatever th' poor saps ahead o' us left layin' about, or... I suppose that we could go divin' intae th' caverns, see what kind of thin' is hauntin', but iffin' all is all th' same tae ye... an ether walk could at least help us tae see iffin' th' killers got nastiness in th' dirt, waitin' on us tae take th'

35

wrong step."

He gave a glum, wordless nod.

"Very. An' I cannae sae that I'm o' any kind o' hurry tae find this critter unprepared, considerin' th' body-count. Really ain't a way tae dae this any kinda approach that'd be completely safe. Without goin' between? We've got th' tool tae dae it. Save us all some pain."

"I can see. I can track it."

"Ain't nae way tae be sure that it'd nae come in behind ye. Or iffin' we get seperated some way or other, if *I'd* have any kindae chance tae see it befer it claimed *me* head, tae."

"True. Dammit." Stannoth rubbed his arms and shivered a little. It was colder here than he was used to, even compared to the chilled tunnels on his side of the world. "What do you need?"

"Tae get intae th' veil?"

"Aye."

"Nae tae much. One person trip tho, me boy – where I be goin', ye ain't gonna be able tae follow."

"Understood," he grunted, leaning against the wall behind him. "Adept at this?"

The dwarf gave him a nod. "It ain't exactly what I'd be callin' fun, but it ain't somethin' that I cannae handle. Iffin' ye really want, ye can be readin' over that stupid book while I'ma off in th' other side o' things."

"Could. Dwarf..."

"Yea?"

"Don't like you."

"Nae much o' a fan of ye, either. Point tae that?"

With another grunt, Stannoth looked away and squeezed his arms together a little tighter. "Shouldn't see there. Nobody should. Not mortals. Not made to."

"Aye, an' ye should be able tae see th' sun. What's th' point, boy?"

"You go, you die? You're lost."

Elrok started to size him up again. Tried to take stock of his worry. "Nae more lost than iffin' we get our throats slit down in th' tunnels. Or up skyward. Or wherever we get sent tae next." After a moment, he really realized what he meant. "Yer worried... really worried an' all. What's got ye so scared about what's past th' veil?"

Stannoth looked back down at him. "The deep dark. I've seen it. You haven't. You had? You'd stay away. Truth."

"Better tae be just me headin' in alone than another raid on th' warren. Worth th' risk. An' even if not fer them, fer us. I dunna fancy bein' sent down tae th' Heart o' th' World just yet an' all. Hopin' ye aren't ready fer it either. Work with me on this, me boy, an' we'll make it through it. Gotta have faith."

"Don't deal in faith. Deal in trust."

"Then ye need tae have trust in th' fact that I ain't ready tae die, an' I'll be careful with meself."

There was a long, pregnant pause, before the archer answered. "That's fair." He looked back at the warren's courtyard where Bayetta and Fanim waited. "Do it."

Elrok tried not to groan when he looked back and saw the two feuding dwarves, well, feuding. "Maybe Bayetta or someone canna show ye wherever they stashed th' stuff yer lady-kin an' th' other hunters left behind? Really, me boy. I'll be okay iffin' ye ain't watchin' o'er me."

"Can't fight there," he argued. "End up dead. You should be watched."

"But outside th' circle, I'ma safe."

"Don't know that."

"I dae. These are me folk."

"Your dead folk."

"Well, yea. But, we've an advantage."

Stannoth tried to read him and couldn't. "What?"

"They ain't gonna know what all I'll be layin' down as traps when I carve in an' down th' spell circle."

"Don't trust them? Thought you did."

"Trust? Nae, nae much more than a lil'. We all lie, an' I *really* ain't in nae mood tae join th' departed."

"Your call."

"Aye. It is."

"Fine."

"We got a plan then?"

"Yes. We do."

"We need tae tell 'em."

"Damn."

"Aye, that."

When they re-entered the square, the girl raised her hand to stop them from saying anything. "I know ye gave up th' throne an' all, Underprince. But there ain't a one o' us that dunna know what kinda trainin' ye got. It's why I called for ye by name."

"And me?" Stannoth asked.

"As I said. Ye've got th' sight, and ye've got th' reputation on yer shoulders. I dunna know about anythin' yer kin have fer standards an' function. I'ma sorry fer that. An', fer what it's worth, I found out sh' went topside befer sh' passed. I dunnae think that sh' talked tae any o' th' locals up there or whatnot." She gave a fresh glare at the Gemwarden. "Seems that someone had 'is pupil go with 'er tae get 'er outta 'is beard."

The archer stared back at Fanim. There was more there, he was absolutely sure of it. "She return with anything?"

"Oh, some tripe about some nomad types fightin' each other. Idiots. Likely th' humans responsible fer puttin' that tusker down 'ere," he answered. "Vestalic? Boy didn't say a damned thin' about it when I asked 'im."

Bayetta's glare spoke volumes. "As soon as I heard that's where sh' was lookin' fer answers, I got word passed tae th' right people topside tae get ye both summoned. Anythin' from th' tunnels? We can take down damned near all o' it. Somethin' from up above? We ain't exactly experts on monsters that dunnae dig. An' with one o' yer folk tryin' tae rest peacefully now... We know yer stomach fer revenge. Yer skills, yer fire. Iffin' sh' went tae th' sky, then sh' must've had a good reason, one that idiot couldn't figure. 'Tis why I asked for ye, truly."

"Understood. Thank you."

"Nae. Thank ye, suncursed. Ye dae whatcha think ye need tae dae. Whatever Fanim ain't be willin' tae help ye out with, I promise, I'll be gettin' it tae ye."

The Gemwarden rapped his cane against the ground. "Ye've nae right tae dae a damned thin' that I dunna tell ye that ye can dae. I'm willin' tae provide a lil' fer Elrok. I ain't willin' tae throw th' keys tae th' blasted warren off tae a *damian*. We cannae solve this on our own. Ain't nae reason tae give up jus' yet."

"Your people die. I don't care. Killed a Nightshade. Killed hunters. Now I care. Don't want keys. Don't want the tunnels. I have a job. Help or not. Your choice." Stannoth finally snapped. He was struggling to keep from kicking him. Ideally someplace soft. With a really, really, really, *hard* kick.

Elrok begrudgingly agreed with his partner and Bayetta. "Fanim, somethin's gotta be done. We know it, ye know it. Let us dae our job."

He looked like he was going to put up a fight. After a few tense moments, he sighed and hung his head. "As ye wish, Underprince. I've nae will tae ever get intae yer business, so dunna expect a lotta help from me. *I've* gotta job tae deal with tae *actually* solve this problem. An' we will."

"Nae ye won't, ye pompous brat," Bayetta growled. "Cause iffin' ye coulda've, we'd not buryin' so many o' us every day."

"Enough," Stannoth growled. "Elrok wants the veil. I want her logbook. Where is it?"

"An' where dae ye have a place fer me tae get setup at?"

The youngest dwarf smiled at him. "I'll be seein' tae it, huntsmen. Jus' follow me."

That made up his mind: for the first time in his life, he might like a dwarf. Didn't trust her, but...

Would wonders never cease.

III. THE VEIL AND THINGS BEFORE AND BEYOND

Their newest companion wormed her way though far too many tunnels and hallways for Stannoth to feel comfortable. It was significantly bigger than he had expected; what he had thought was just a small outpost had a number of interesting amenities. The "town square" they had been in was just... a rally point.

The warren proper had at least two more of those open plazas that that he saw as they they passed through and so much more. He thought he even saw a glimmering crystal cavern, but for reasons yet unknown, the two of them were pushed past it in a hurry. *More secrets. I'll regret this. Every day I live.*

In short order he came to the realization that they had built it for full-scale subterranean warfare. Something was down here that they wanted to protect. Or maybe had wanted to protect years before. Whatever the cause, whatever the reason? Anything that wanted to take Kepershal by force would have to send an army a thousand-strong to have a chance to break through the labyrinth... let alone anything else.

It gave him an idea. And he didn't like it.

No army. One, two, attackers. Could do it. That orc? Might do it, he mused to himself.

While she wouldn't give him a full history of the warren, citing only "th' orcs," at least she was able to confirm that yes, they had preserved the gear of the fallen damian. It was the only good news that she had. Bayetta told him as much about her as she could, even if it wasn't much.

Stannoth's kin had shown up without warning or invitation. She stayed out of the way of her hosts and spent time deeper in the tunnels in places that they really hadn't explored. She had asked questions, but by all accounts, nobody had wanted to give her any answers. They were told that she had tried to ask Fanim for more information after she came back from her trip topside... but, the Gemwarden hadn't bothered to tell her a thing.

Neither hunter was surprised.

By the time that they arrived at their destination – a nearly hidden, out of the way temple – they both had everything that they could hope to be told. Nothing new jumped out at either one of them, leaving the trip to the veil the only real option left.

Upon their arrival into it, there wasn't a lot to do other than to prepare the room for Elrok's spell. Thankfully, luckily, it didn't take a lot of preparation to set it up. Still, it gave time for one last question. Not about the murders, but about the murdered.

"Why wait? Why would they linger?" Stannoth asked. It had been nagging at him since they had brought up the idea. The Veil served to act as a buffer between this world and the next. Not much dwelled there, although the things that did were not typically friendly. Not even to each other. By nature of the realm, they couldn't do anything to each other... but they just weren't 'friendly.'

"Well. Me people dunnae tend tae wander tae much, even in death. It's a tad easier fer us, bein' so close tae th' world. We're truly deep down, children o' th' land. Dirt, rock, an' all that."

His partner struggled with the concept. "Dirt keeps them?"

"We ain't in any hurry tae find out where we be headed. Ain't nobody should be." He scratched at his chin. "Some o' us 'ave figured that it's a tad safer just tae keep a feel fer our home in th' ever-after."

"Brave."

"Or stupid," Elrok answered. "Cannae say that I'd wanna tae stick around over there. I ain't never seen anythin' that look likes it'd be so awesome in th' things that hover between. When I'm dead an' gone? I'll be happy tae move on."

Bayetta looked into the chapel and shrugged. "Desperation. Canna make any soul nae wish tae leave what they know an' all."

As he crafted a circle in chalk at their feet, the diminutive hunter looked up at his partner. "I know why yers stick around in th' Shadewells. Hidin' from judgment... hidin' from a lot, iffin' th' stories be told tae us be true. Why are ye so surprised about our folk wantin' tae stick around on this side o' the ether?"

"The caves are misery. A prison. No warmth. No light. The havens have more."

"An' th' pits have piss-all less."

"Righteous don't fear that."

The dwarf crinkled his nose."Suppose so, suppose so," the short hunter sighed. "Cannae say I'd be blamin' 'em yer people fer not wantin' tae risk th' afterlife, fer sure. Not after what all's gone on about in this one. Yer folks got th' bad side o' that deal. Ain't nae way tae tell iffin' there's more tae it on th' other side."

"Wasn't a deal."

Elrok gave a shrug. "Well, whatever it is it was. Th' lot of ye sure as all piss paid fer it. Cannae see th' sun? Quite literally, cannae see it without dyin'? That's a curse that's all kindae wrong. I know yer kin an' mine don't exactly get along so well but I've never thought yer folk got anythin' but fisked o'er it."

"We did. So. What needs done?" the taller of the two asked, dropping the topic while waving his hand at the mess of upturned chairs and tables scattered amongst the shrine. It looked like it had been raided and ransacked; empty alcoves were devoid of their idols, pews pushed away and scattered. Empty, dust-free spots on the walls showed where paintings and rugs had once hung to honor the Gods and Godlings of the dwarves. Apparently when they left they had simply grabbed as much as they could and ran.

That wasn't far from the truth. "They even took down th' effigy o' th' Stonehewn? Our patron? These poor people. Tae even so much as move that is tae risk th' wrath o' th' land, let alone take it outta 'ere an' send it topside. Ye know, I dunna have a damned clue at fisk all about what coulda have gone through 'ere an' done so much damned damage but I'ma gonna tell ye right now, I ain't gonna shed a tear when I strip its skin from bone."

"In time. If it has skin. Or bones. What needs done?" Stannoth asked again. He didn't really like to repeat himself, but it was hard to argue with Elrok's frustration.

With a sigh, the smaller huntsman looked around. After a few brief moments of instruction, the pair went to work while Bayetta took a quiet inventory of the shrine. They didn't entirely work in silence but there wasn't a lot of chatter between them. Not until they had cleared out a large section in the middle of the floor and the dwarf started pulling supplies out of his belt pouches, that was.

"I know ye ain't exactly what one'd called thrilled with this an' all, Stanny. But. I've gone through 'ere, done this an' that befer. I ain't callin' on a Godling type tae bless me soul an' guide me hand on some pile o' fluff an' feathers. Nae any deals within somethin' that'd wanna take me soul or some bodily sacrifice."

The damian looked at the items that his companion was stacking up. Some kind of sulfuric chalk, channeling crystals, and some kind small metal idol that he was carefully unwrapping.

"No divine? Then why the icon?" he asked, pointing at the figure. It was scuffed but still shiny, chrome in the light.

Elrok grinned. "There's a toll tae be paid. Kings an' queens ain't th' only ones with taxmen that come tae pass."

"Paying in idols?"

"Nae," he said with that same grin. "But th' statue melts down but nice an' can be used iffin' I'm ever a few coins short an ale." The remark caught a grunt of a laugh from the archer before he realized he was doing it. "Th' spells take it. Dunna know what it actually does tae it, but, it takes it."

"Sounds like a sacrifice."

Scratching at his arm, the dwarf paused for a moment. "Well... dunnae know tae who it'd be tae."

"Reassuring."

While he watched, the dwarf raked the chalk over the floor in a quarter-dozen interlocking circles and then triangles. The setup itself took less than ten minutes of effort before he pushed the tools aside and sat down in the center of it all. "Ye've seen this befer, yea?"

"Aye. Spell suspends your body. Your soul leaves. It enters the veil. It isn't like here. Dark. Cold. Quiet. Just etheric remnants there. Circle is the anchor. Body the tether. Can't interact with us. See, float, fly. No physical barriers. Some magical ones. Spell ends on your return. You can control that. Ends when you say. No set time. Spell breaks before that? Body destroyed, murdered? You're lost forever. Awful fate. Still shouldn't do it."

It was, without question, the most that anyone had heard the damian say the entire time since he had entered the tunnels. It somehow surprised the shorter one; he didn't think he had it in him. "Alright me boy. Then all I canna tell ye is that I'll be back in a time. Try not tae dae anythin' that ye'd get killed fer while I'm on me way out, would ye?"

If he could glare, he would have. The rest of his face was enough to get the message across. "Get it done."

Laughing, Elrok made one more mark on the floor and set the fabric around the idol on fire. "Be good an' all!" he said as it melted into nothingness, and then the magic happened. Unexpectedly (and unnoticed) it just wasn't the magic that he wanted or had planned. Behind him, and outside of view of either Hunter, part of the ground moved and shifted. Symbols rearranged themselves as the rocks they were on lifted and slid away. Before the dwarf could cast his spell, the spell was changed...

...and then the *unintended* magic happened.

Elrok's form waxed and waned in the circle. A steady wind churned inside it. The dwarf was lifted and slowly spun around in the air. The soldiers sent to guard them watched on with complete and utter fascination. His companion was less impressed.

He stayed and watched for the first hour. Nothing changed in the circle and nothing came out of it. Whatever he was doing in there wasn't showing in his flesh. Stannoth still loathed the idea, but he supposed that it was a good sign. When the hour crested and the dwarf hadn't returned, his curiosity finally got the better of him. A few short words to Bayetta, and she lead him back into the warren proper and off to the nursery they had stored the Nightshade's belongings in. When he asked why, she simply said that the woman had felt a connection to the children and stayed at their side, even after a trio of them all turned up dead at once.

Even with the minimal courtesy that had been provided to the lost damian, they had at least tried to keep her equipment in as best condition as they could. It was absolutely obvious that she hadn't died a pleasant death. They had kept her cloak and some of her clothes (that they were torn and bloody was to say the least). Even her shortsword was cracked down the entire length of the blade. Whatever it hit had to have been harder than steel.

If she had brought any charms or relics, they were gone. The only other things that stood out were an empty belt pouch and a knapsack that had a blanket, canteen, assorted eating utensils, and lockpicks. Even her rations were missing.

In other words, it was a depressing sight that gave him almost no idea what had happened until he found his prize. On the surface, the journal was just that - a journal. It named her as Lessiana Tei'mara, from the Walthershen Enclave. He'd never traveled that far himself; however, they *were* known for their contact with the Deepshadows. It was an interesting development. They *weren't* known for getting involved the affairs of distant lands.

Among other things, every last one of them were worshipers of the Great Reaper. That fact didn't lend them to playing nice with others. Anyone that knew about them flat-out avoided them just for that reason. It wasn't an unwise decision.

Why would she? he mused. They *hated* outsiders; dwarves? Even moreso.

It was just another mystery to solve. Hopefully the easiest one.

He had to peel some of the pages apart; they were splattered with blood, and they stuck together. Less than a good sign. You would think that Stannoth would have a hard time reading through the book with the metal over his eyes. But, the magic itself wasn't that cruel. As with the other things, it let him see it clearly he could read it almost as easily as anyone else.

The first half of it were just thoughts and remarks about her life and her time in her tunnels and the areas nearby. It wasn't her history and ramblings that were important – no, it was what she had hidden between the lines using magic that only another damian would recognize or could even read. The first line told him all he needed to know. *"Do not trust."* It really wasn't hard to guess who or what. The next part was just worse: *"DEATH TAKES US ALL!"*

Journal Entry, 5th of Tasslin's Joy
By request of the Darkfather, I will be leaving for the Kepershal Gem Warren come the next tide. I do not know what it is he has divined, only that the shadows have spoken. He has told me I am to help the short ones at any cost. He wishes the truce be honored between our peoples. Yet, there is more. He looks troubled. He is troubled. He was truly insistent, yet, truly vague. We had no messengers nor envoys from the Crystal Kingdom in the days preceding his order.

Still, he was as sure that our aid is as needed as I am sure life needs water. I communed with the void for guidance, and in its silence, I feel that the path before me is my fate. May the Peace of Death guide me to warm shadows, and the soft breath of dusk.

Journal Entry, 12th of Tasslin's Joy
I have arrived at Kepershal. The shadows have reason to be distraught. Too many are dead. I see the ripples of too many souls not long past. Investigation is absolutely warranted. I know nothing, but I will see everything. The dark here growls at me; it is not just that there are dead, there is... death. In all my times taught and teaching those that have passed before me, I've yet to feel something quite like this. I will attempt to summon one of the lost tomorrow, but I do not believe any will answer.

Journal Entry, 13th of Tasslin's Joy
I was correct. No souls reached for me when I put my hand in their world. Did they flee? Were they cast to judgment? Consumed by the opposition that stalks the shadows? With nary a body to be had, there is not enough to command a spirit to depart their fate in the after – no matter what their after may be. I will move to other options tomorrow.

Journal entry, 14th of Tasslin's Joy
I am not alone in knowing nothing. The dwarves are equally as

clueless. *Oddly shocking, most welcomed me. I would be surprised, but they are desperate for answers. I think they would have welcomed a troll should one come bearing wisdom. Fifteen now dead, no wounded, and no understanding.*

Gemwarden Fanim was angry that I had come uninvited. His Geomancer wasn't much happier, but he provided counsel to not have me executed or sent upon my way. They are the only two that have objected to my arrival... so, for now, I feel safe.

There is much hidden in these tunnels. I see that there may be more than simply one cause. The aura reeks of deep magic. Old magic. Something cursed lives in this land. I feel that it has been here longer than these dwarves. THESE dwarves – the halls hum with the memories of ones that lived here long before the ones that now claim it as their home. Ancestors, mayhaps, or simply a tribe that built this home and left it long ago.

Yet still, even with murders fresh in the dust and bodies ages-old deep in the stone, still no spirit answers my call.

Journal Entry, 15th of Tasslin's Joy
I was wrong. The troll wasn't as welcome as expected.

Journal Entry, 19th of Tasslin's Joy
I have begun to question the history of the Gemwarren. Although this outpost is not far from the borders of the Qualechi Dwarves, there is no evidence to be seen that there were ever any infighting in these tunnels in recent years, let alone recent weeks. Those cannibals have nothing to do with this. Another threat easily dismissed. Still. These dwarves are hiding so much. They are open, but maddeningly defensive and protective. How am I to help them? How am I to honor the truce? If they do not be honest with me, then what hope do I have to save them?

Journal Entry, 20th of Tasslin's Joy
I... I am shaken. I discovered children dead this day. Three, little ones. They were cold to the touch. So cold. I saw the fear on their faces. It was etched there. Carved into each of their eyes and their lips. I have never seen such terror. Not even in the depths of the Olddark. I have supped with the ghosts of men that have been dined upon by creatures born of the blackest of eternities, and their fear is nothing to what I have seen carved into the faces of these children.

The community is on the edge of revolt. Their Gemwarden is trying to mute this. He is trying to keep me from seeing how upset his people are. I do not know if he will permit me to stay for much longer. His desire for power in the face of this is disgusting. I will seek audience with the Shades of Long Past tonight, should they heed my call and allow me to enter their otherworldly court between the worlds.

My anger grows at the cavalier attitude presented by the "leaders" of this warren. Even if they should not deign to truly wish to find the cause of this butchery, I will – and I will drag it from here and stake it out under the light for all to flay.

Journal Entry, 23rd of Tasslin's Joy

I may not have found a source of the deaths but I have found something interesting. The Shades instructed me to search well outside of here, that there was something crawling through the caves that did not belong. As I scoured the tunnels, I encountered a creature. Human, in form. Barely. It had no mind and little else. It is not dead but it there is no reason for it not to be. It reeks of pure death even as it shambles through life seemingly and disturbingly immortal. It is not a young soul, despite the appearance of an otherwise youthful body. Not only is it not dead, it seems to have transcended life.

The aura is wrong. Alien. Not of this world, and in all of my travels, I have never seen such a creature that has existed in this world nor the next. It is that it is human, in a place no humans should be. It is not native to the tunnels but it has gone mad within them. You may remove the man from the sun but the touch of the sun on the skin will not so easily fade.

Yet even more so strange is that I see that he is not from far away from here. He is not a stranger to the land... only the underlands. I have given him to the short ones. I've no further use of it. There is more deeper in. I will find it. Perhaps to go below, I will need to search above. At least it will free me of these tunnels... do these rodents never bathe?

Journal Entry, 28th of Tasslin's Joy

These dwarves are fools! They live their lives under the ground, having forsaken the sun, throwing away all of their care of what happens on the surface. They were chased under the stone in generations past, but they could always leave it without risk or fear, and yet they refuse that gift! They care for so little, and they ignore all but what they have to! Vestalic, the Gemwarden's pupil, was thrown to me to serve as a guide through the dankest caves in the furthest edges of the tunnels. He is a miserable, insufferable little man, even for a dwarf. He never took his eyes off of me. Stared, the entire time.

Disturbing. If it had continued, he would have disappeared... purely by accident. Surely the Abyss would welcome him? Nobody else would.

The fool couldn't even find the way out that he himself had espoused and swore was there! Ended up lost in the tunnels. If we had been attacked, I'd have had no way of running from it, should the worst happen. He was so pathetically worried.

Disgusting worm. Then he let it slip that he knew how to use rock-portals. We wandered for three days, and **then** *he remembered? I detest this place! But that is not important. What is was the realm outside. Oh, and what a surface did I find! They don't* **know**? *They don't* **care**! *Half of their answers can be found just outside! That fool was as surprised as I when we found the source of the 'immortality' magic. He stood there, lost and stunned! Barely moved! The idiot! Damn the fools!*

This warren is beneath the Midland Wastes! Were you to ask me of a worse place to be steeped in ill magic in the midst of all of the kingdoms and city states in the western continent, I wouldn't be able to give you one. Yet they are surprised to find that there is pain and suffering here! SURPRISED! I would be more surprised if there wasn't. Fools. For all their surviving in strife with the orcs and goblins and gnolls and the creatures in the lower-darks, they have no idea how to handle the magics of the over-realms.

The men above them have been cursed with immortality. Never to age, never to die, always to war with each other. It is what they do. Gifted by the God of War to never fall to entropy. That is the fate of the maddened soul I found. Their curse is to war and never fall! To offend the Great Reaper by always living through death! They fight each other in the name of their God and have no fear of the next world because for them, there is none! That is the above.

This is the down here. It should not be down this far and it should not be this far from home. It must have gotten lost? I saw those men above. They are not maddened like this. They are not steeped in death and wounds. They are as sane as I and wiser than these fools under them.

That creature has been cut off. Tortured and driven insane. I was not able to speak to any of the warriors on the surface, only observe. I do not dare ask them for help; their war could come below. What would happen to the rest of the short ones if it did? Or the men above? Would they be crazed if taken from the over-realms? Does the magic that keeps them alive there change when they come down here? If it isn't that... if the removal of the sun is not what causes this sickness....? What creature could kill so many, drive the immortal mad, and leave no trace but death?

Where could it have come from to stalk these caves?

Journal Entry, 1st of Radian

I spoke to the hunters that arrived. Gutter-spawned mercenaries. I detest them, but they do have their uses. I do not see myself ever working with them; vermin, a symptom of the corruption of the Kingdoms of Man. More of this story now comes together. Hired by a human trading company... Blackstone. I know of those men. I saw their banners overland. They are there, in the midst of the immortals. Their Lord claims to serve gold, but in truth, he is a willing servant of the Great Reaper. It is a secret from many.

But the Darkfather knows. He has always known. Now I do as well. The Blackstone war with the immortals. Actively, they trade blows today, now even, Death against War. The shadows scream in pain. They act through agents of their causes... and now, I know. Death seeks to bring true peace, the only true peace. War, to fight any and all for all eternity. The true foe of War is that it ends when the last heart stops beating; so to conquer that? To overcome that one insurmountable event? War may be offended by Death but Death would not care until – unless! - it was removed from the field of battle. It was.

Now, it seems, the Reaper has made plans to gather an overripe harvest. There are other actors in that story; I can feel it. One borne of Love, one borne of Rage, one of... one of a different kind of Dark. I do not believe that they are important, not to... not to this matter. To others, yes, but not this matter.

With luck it will stay that way. These tunnels do not need more grief to flood into them. Such a war above could truly have repercussions for below. If there is but a chance that there is a creature loosed by the Reaper to cull the immortals... if it could not follow its nature... this, this may be the cause, the catalyst. I know that eternity comes for us all. Now, mayhaps, it has grown impatient.

I will present this to the Gemwarden come what passes for day in this mildewing cavern with pretentious airs. An agent of the Great Reaper is not a thing to be trifled with. More bodies will follow if he does not send all of his kin far from here. This will take a great deal of magic to contain, if it is as I think. It may take more than I have on my own. Maybe... maybe I will make an exception to working with the huntsmen after all.

Journal Entry, 2nd of Radian

The Gemwarden will not listen. He won't send them away. It's only a matter of time befo

Bloodstains covered the rest of the page. The fake entries stopped at this point as well. The next few pages were empty save for dark blotches of what he hoped was just blood. When he finally found more of her remarks, the words were scrawled about everywhere. Stannoth's mouth went dry as he felt the urgency in her writing, the pain that filled each word.

...massacre... the hunters, dead, three more dwarves... something came out of the wall... and a new actor... don't know on who's behalf... she cut the heads from two... immortals. Hurt... hurt one of the dwarves. Stuck her hand in his throat... nearly... ripped it out... but... No blood. Sand. It was sand. She saved me. Claws, she had claws. I don't know what it is that claims these lives. It has to be close by. Or another doing... its bidding. A traitor to the dwarves... could be any... ran, I ran, keep running can't con... it won't go down, I hid, I ran I hid, can't put it... won't fall to the pit, tried hard, safe for... now, safe now RUN IF YOU SEE THIS RUN.

The last entry wasn't just bloodstained. It was shredded. A gash had been ripped almost all the way through it to the back of the book. A bloody chunk of dirt fell out from the back of the last page. All he could imagine was that whatever had caught her had left her for dead, and the final words were a desperate last warning:

He nt lke he othrs. Not immorl... anmited... girl ct his thrt away... saw... stone dirt repaired... poured from... DEATH IS IT IS IT... Shdows sav ME, shadws com for no dows, my baby lov my...!

The dwarf Bayetta had assigned to help him was pacing back and forth behind him, in and out of the doorway... almost enough to drive the damian to distraction. Despite that, he did serve to give him warning, however brief. Not enough of one, but he did give it. When the guard suddenly stopped moving, there was a brief moment of silence before Stannoth noticed and began to wonder why.

When he turned his head, he saw it. It was what had claimed so many lives. The monster that had stalked the tunnels. It was so very easy to see how, and how it had stayed hidden for so long. *It* was a cloud of sand.

Floating, moving, apparently sentient, sand.

There really wasn't any way that its next victim could have moved even if he had wanted to. He tried, oh he tried to fight, but it didn't help. He couldn't even scream before dust and almost white sand flowed out of the stonework at his feet and out of the walls. It smothered him; suffocated him. It lifted him up into the air, suspended on a pillar of rocky dirt. Bow in hand, all Stannoth could do was watch the murder and scramble to think of a spell or potion (or weapon) that he could use to stop it.

He managed a curse, briefly, before a stone hand shot out of the wall and grabbed him by the throat. He had time to realize that this was a new creature, something summoned, before it started to squeeze, and his already-fogged sight began to fail him. Someone entered the room as it shoved him bodily against a wall.

The impact made his world go black.

Interestingly enough, at the exact same moment, Elrok's world was starting to go *white*...

Inside the veil, the world was different. It was the same but it was still... not. Shapes and bodies were less than solid. He could see through and past them. He saw Bayetta's aura first; a dwarf of unusually pronounced beauty (at least to him – the thoughts of the tasteless damian be damned, whatever they were) in the physical world and a softly glowing symbol of joy in this. He was almost afraid to look at his coworker, but when he did, he was dumbfounded by what he saw.

The man was an innocent. He had blood in his aura, a lot of blood. No doubt about it - he was a killer. But he still had purity. He had honor, he had honesty. And still, part of him was pure. Whatever doubts the dwarf may have had about his character or his intentions were gone the second he saw the soft and calming ripples in the ether that the damian left behind every time he drew a breath. To say that it was unexpected would be an understatement.

When he got back, he told himself he'd make much more of an effort to be much less of a pain.

There was also something around him. A fog around his head, a gray shroud, almost opaque. It instantly explained why he had been having such a hard time since entering the warren. What Elrok had dismissed as shoddy spellwork cast by the bottom-feeding cave moss that dared to call themselves "enchanters" in the damian tunnels? No, that fog was the result of an intentionally-cast hex that muted Stannoth's sight as efficiently as a sack cloth hood. Not only did he feel bad for being dismissive, being *wrong* about him pissed him off at the same time. Someone had bespelled him, ripping away his most useful tool to do his job (let alone to live his life).

Bloody lovely. Now he owed him an apology. *Absolutely bloody lovely*, he growled.

Getting back required getting something else done first. Once he quit being a spiritual voyeur and turned away from the shrine, he saw things that weren't quite right. Little shades fluttered out of the room, through the door, through the walls, and into the alcoves where the idols had been. The problem with removing the marks of the holy was that there were always things that were happy to soak up the energy left behind.

By themselves, they probably weren't a problem. Were they indicative that worse things might be around? Yes. They were a symptom of the problem and weren't unexpected. Having so many of them here so soon after the temple had been abandoned? ...now, *that* was a bit more of a concern. A handful, that would be one thing. A swarm, another.

He felt a ripple outside of the temple and slowly, carefully, made his way through the empty, haunted hallways. Echos of the past rippled through the ocean of ether all around him. Also expected — at times beautiful, at other times scary, but they were expected. They were also useful; seeing where and what had been was as important as seeing what was now.

He could see the remnants of families that had gone to the shrine dutifully every day passing back and forth, overlapping themselves, always sliding through each other, eternally walking through the warren. Echos were harmless. No minds, no souls. Imprints in the ether. They'd fade, in time.

The longer he looked though, he could see something moving through the walls themselves. It shouldn't have been there. It wasn't an echo, and it wasn't a ripple. There were things that lived in the veil, of course, things that nested in the world between worlds. That thing wasn't one of them, shouldn't have been one of them. Whatever it was, it should not have been there.

It was gone before he could get a good look. It just felt *wrong*. What had it been doing in the chapel? His 'skin' went cold at the thought that maybe, just maybe, they should have sent an exorcist instead. Sometimes those holy fiskers *were* a little better equipped...

He didn't get a lot of time to think on it.

The next thing he felt, the next very wrong thing he felt, was the vibration from the scream that came from the pit they had put the wretched human in. He rushed to it the second he felt the prick of the pain from it on his skin, and it, of all the things it was, *innocent* it was not. Angry red energy was wrapped around it. It thrashed and lashed out in the air, leaving deep scores in the soul of the land all around him. It was corrupting everything it touched, and the echos in the room above it had been all but completely eradicated because of it.

In the mortal plane, it could barely make a sound. In here, it screamed in raw agony. It was aware of itself, it was conscious, and it understood its fate. It was lost, it was hurt, and it was tormented.

The pain it was suffering was almost unfathomable. It had gone completely mad. It was not a fate that Elrok envied. Nothing he had ever witnessed suffered as much as this poor, pathetic creature. Nothing even came close. Questioning it in this world was out of the question and with that option gone, it set him back.

It wasn't a total loss. There were tendrils from it that cast echos of their own. Those echos flicked through the halls and back into the warren, deeper into it. With a saddened sigh, the dwarf tracked them through walls and through the stone, hunting them. Those tendrils helped him see the path of another figure, a strong one, moving through the outpost every day.

The very first thing he could see was that it was nearly as tortured as the wretch in the pit. Every place it had gone was twisted in madness, torn asunder with chaos. It had power, uncontrollable power, agonized power. This was the killer he was after. It was blacker than the void and darker than the midnight sky.

He liked it less by the minute.

It had been everywhere. Was everywhere. Inside the warren and... inside the stone? That wasn't right. If it was moving that freely it had to be some kind of spirit. There weren't really any other options that it could have been. At least, that's what he thought until he saw Stannoth and Bayetta walking out of the shrine.

As he watched them travel, his stomach sank. The faint figure he had seen moving through the walls had started to take a more visible form. He had been right; it wasn't an echo, and it didn't look like it was the soul of any dwarf that had ever been. In fact, he hadn't seen any of those at all. His kin weren't here. None of them were. They should have been. There should have been at least one, one disoriented soul out of so many wrongfully dead, there should have been one, but there were just this...

...thing. This thing that walked in the wake of the shadowed killer. It had a long neck with a bulbous, iris-free eye that blinked at him when it saw him floating in the ether. It had four 'legs' that were little more than hooked claws that descended from a bent and oblong trunk. If it had been flesh and blood, it would have clacked on the ground as it walked. It gave him the impression of a kidney with spines.

They stared at each other. This was not right. This was *not* supposed to be here. It didn't have the right aura for a creature that would be able to exist past the veil but it was too... *real* to be able to stay in this realm unaided. It backed away and scurried off. Thankfully. He hadn't seen anything like it before and was pretty damn certain that he never wanted to again.

Life was full of disappointments.

And, honestly, so was the afterlife.

By the time he turned back around to watch the damian and Bayetta, the woman had gone away. At least, that one had. There was another in the room with his companion, and she wasn't a dwarf at all. Nor was she alive. That was the first wraith, the only wraith, that he saw. Nor was she *happy* about her fate. While anger darkened the light around her, she was keeping it muted and directed inward. It both empowered her to stay in this realm and kept her hidden from anyone who would wish her gone.

It was an impressive level of self control. For one of her training, it wasn't really hard at all. She hovered in front of Stannoth, flinging her spirit to and fro, doing all in her power she could do to get him to see her.

"Listen, listen, listen, please, listen, don't sit don't wait listen, listen, listen, listen..." she chanted again and again and again. *"I know you see, I see, I know, the magic in your face I see, I know, I listen, you listen, listen, listen, please, listen, don't sit don't wait listen, listen, listen, SEE ME, LISTEN! Why can't you SEE ME or LISTEN!"* she cried.

For whatever reason, he didn't respond. He should have. The magic that let him see through the metal covering his eyes should have. It didn't. The fog was doing its job, and it was doing it exceedingly well. "Lady, th' boy is blinded. He cannae see much past 'is feet without havin' a right struggle."

She whipped her head back and took quick stock of him. *"Damn dwarf! Why did you do this to him? To me? To us! Came to aid you! You cursed us! You killed me will kill him! WHY?!"*

Why did the dead always have to be so damn... cranky?

Elrok floated away a little bit from her. "Lady. I dunna dae a damn thin' tae ye or 'im. We're 'ere tae help, all we're both after. Yer th' one that came 'ere ahead o' 'im, yea? Th' Nightshade?"

The soul looked down at Stannoth while he fished out a battered book from her belongings. *"Doesn't matter. You. You have to go. Go now. He'll be dead. Dead if you don't. GO! Save him! Be quick, he comes!"*

"Dead? Th' boy is safe an' all. There ain't a thin' in there but us, and we ain't exactly capable o' cuttin' th' boy down about now. Iffin' ye can tell me somethin' about what happened we might be able tae -"

"HE COMES. Go you have to go you have to go or he'll be trapped here, we'll both be trapped here HE COMES here HERE he is HERE now! Dead in dirt! Dead in world! END in HERE!"

The dwarf spat out a curse as he looked around the nursery without seeing a damn thing. "Lady! Listen tae me – there's nary a thin' 'ere but ye and me!"

"DEAD MAN IN RED! HE COMES! RUN OR BE WORSE THAN ME WORSE THAN HIM WORSE THAN US NEVER SAFE COME FOR US YOU MUST GO NOW YOU MUST STOP SAND MUST RUN FROM THE RED!!!"

Elrok tried to calm here again, to no avail. "Lady! There ain't be nothin' 'ere tae cause a bit o' pain tae anyone, nae ye, nae th' blind one, nae even me! Ye gotta say what it is! We wanna kill it! Set this shit right an' all!"

She screamed wordlessly at him before suddenly *expanding* to take up the entire room for a heartbeat. Then, just as quickly, she shrank into nothingness and vanished into her journal. Frustrated, Elrok rubbed his chin, and for a moment, wished he could feel the stubble on it. Between the lack of solid, well, anything, and the insanity-muddled spirit, his patience for the day was just about completely gone.

Then he discovered she wasn't wrong, and what was left of his patience changed to raw dread.

The shadow that he had seen earlier slipped into the hallway from behind his companion. It was still cloudy and still opaque as solid rock, but it was definitely there, awake, and focused. It was more than a shadow. It was living darkness. Ripples of magic moved through the ground at its feet, and the guard who was watching out for the damian suddenly seized up as something coiled around it and sucked its life into nothing.

Absolutely nothing. It didn't so much as leave a faint trace of life at all. He saw the soul of the poor man glimmer in the air above it. Then it too was gone, blown to nothing by the swirling vortex that had claimed it. He stopped himself before he made a sound (if but barely) though all he wanted to do was drown the world in screamed profanities.

Horrified, Elrok turned and willed himself through the warren as quick as his mind would let him. He had to get to Stannoth before it was too late. He should have listened to the wraith, he should have been faster he should have...

...he should have run when he first saw the inky creature that had stared him down before.

It was back, and it was not alone. No less than *five* of them materialized through the walls. In unexpected panic, Elrok started to cast the spell to return to the physical world. That was when he realized something else was wrong. He couldn't *will* himself back to his body. He couldn't feel the tether. Something had gone wrong. Something had gone *terribly* wrong.

The leading creature stalked him. A mouth appeared across its midriff, chattering at him. The soul-render started to lunge at him while the dwarf tried to think of *anything* he could do to defend himself. Mortals couldn't fight in the veil, they didn't have the strength, the ability; it wasn't supposed to be a place where things could hurt each other. It was truly a neutral territory. Nothing could cause harm in it; that's what they were taught, that's what *everyone* was always taught. Either the veil was failing (an impossibility; an idea well beyond his ability to fully comprehend) or...

...or it wasn't the veil any longer.

As he realized that, on all sides of the cave, the warren melted away. Shadows vanished as cold light filled the halls. The halls evaporated into a sea of frozen sands, unbroken for as far as the eyes could see. The monster lunged at him as pincers grew from under the 'eye'. It snapped at him, growling, as did the other creatures behind it – all of them making mocking little screams that mimicked Elrok's screamed curses.

Salivating, it lunged for him – and shattered into chunks of inky gravel.

Elrok stood there, petrified, color draining from his face. "*Must run from the red!*" *s*he had said. He had thought she was just lost in the world, lost in her own mind. Suddenly he realized that she might have been right. He should have run. Then he realized that it was too damn late now to even try.

A man in a blood-red robe stood where the monstrosity had been. He flicked bits of the obsidian-like corpse through his fingers and watched it fall to the sand and vanish. The other renderers scattered and dove into the sand, running away as fast as they could. He looked over at the hunter, looked him up and down, and then unleashed a deeply irritated sigh of long-suffering.

"Well, now. *Another* little lost dwarf. Oh, how *lucky* me."

Rough, scratchy stones ground against Stannoth's throat as they lifted him up into the air. Impossibly, supernaturally strong, the creature pulled itself free of the bricks at his back and the granite at his feet. No, that wasn't right; it *was* a creature made of rocks. The only thing his addled brain could think was either a golem or some kind of stone elemental... before it drove him down into and through one of the nursery beds to the floor below.

Chunks of dull quartz bit into him through his chainmail and ripped the leather padding underneath to shreds. Slowly, the creature lumbered around until it was between the hunter and its master. Whatever it was had a head but no face; a body, but nothing flesh. Much of it looked like it was only held together by that same sentient sand that had attacked the guard.

"Ye shouldn't've come 'ere, ye shouldn't've. Ye got warned, warned away topside, ye coulda, ye shoulda stayed away, this didn't have tae be," a dwarf babbled at him from the other side of the room.

Clutching at the rock, Stannoth wasn't able to say a word, and could just make agonized choking sounds. It twisted him on the broken bed while it tilted its own faceless head side to side. It was looking at him. It was... studying him. Looking for something.

It wasn't alone. Unable to respond to the murderer controlling it, Stannoth *looked* into the aura of the beast. Fog or not, it was close enough to see into it, even if he couldn't see *what* the other thing was. It wasn't just one thing; it was two things. A pair of entities mixed into one. The rock was just that - a rock — but animated, sentient, and a literal creature of the land. The other thing...

The yammering dwarf continued on and interrupted his battered train of thought. "Ye did find somethin' now, didn't ye? Dammit. Just... damn ye. Trying so hard, can't ye see it? Tryin', always tryin', tryin' tae save 'er. An' that bitch. Sh' almost ruined it. Ruined it all. Couldn't. Couldn't let 'er die like th' others. Had tae make it look worse, make it scare everyone off. Make it look like maybe Fanim did 'er in. Get yer people tae kill '*im*, not be lookin' fer me. But ye did. Ye found me, an' I shoulda sent ye intae th' rocks when I could've."

The deranged dwarf was pacing back and forth near the door. He wasn't taking any risks about getting near his next would-be victim, and the elemental wasn't letting up on the damian at all. He tried to turn to look at him but he couldn't quite see him, yet. Not yet. He could reach into part of his cloak, though - and that was a start.

He simply wasn't sure if he could survive to the finish.

"I told Fanim, told 'im, told 'im we had tae toss it out. Toss it all out with 'er. '*No*,' 'e said. '*Ain't right tae take all o' 'er from 'er own kin. Not th' honorable thin' tae dae.*' Honor?" Whoever it was scampered closer. Stannoth could almost recognize the voice. "*Honor?* Nobody cared a damn about *honor* when sh' got trapped. Nary a damned soul. Coulda let 'er dae what she had tae dae. No! Caved th' ground in on 'er. Imprisoned 'er!"

As the damian started to go slack and stopped struggling, the golem started to relax its grip. He was finally able to turn his head enough to see who had turned on his own kind. When he did, it didn't help him understand why, although now some of his statements made (a little) more sense. "You... Geo... Geomancer?" he croaked out.

Vestalic, the one in Lessiana's journal. The one that had sent the hunters down from the quarry above. If anyone could summon the elemental, he could. Rock magic was all they did and a stray thought from the war reminded him that the golden armor he wore meant he was damn good at it. But... *why?*

He wasn't even anything special to look at. Mud-colored hair, dark gray eyes, a nose that looked like it had been broken decades ago, and teeth more broken and jagged than the crib that was tearing into Stannoth's back. He wasn't even taller than Elrok, and the damian thought that stack of muscle wasn't much taller than a glorified pixie at best.

"Oh, now ye, now, now! Someone pays attention tae me. Nobody listened! Nobody! When I first said that all o' 'em needed tae run? Nae. Nae a damned one. Could've saved so many o' 'em iffin' they had just done as I told 'em. Nobody ever thought tae listen tae old Vestalic. Not th' people, not me teacher, not a one. An' now? Tae many dead, an' they could've gone an' been safe, but sh' had tae feed. She *had* tae!"

The damian struggled for words. Too many questions, with next-to-no air to ask. With the anger on his face changing to something else, something wild eyed, something even more frantic, the geomancer gestured at the golem, but Stannoth interrupted him before he could say anything to the stone monstrosity "Killed... how?"

"I let 'er play." Vestalic shot him a look of bewilderment. "But I had tae. They wouldn't go. An' sh' needs tae feed. M'lady needs tae feed. Sh's hurtin'. Hurtin' horrid. Ain't a damn thin' I can dae but tae feed 'er. Sh' even gave up 'er own strength tae help me, help me stay alive. Ye see it? Ye see what one o' yer crazy people did tae me?" he rambled, moving close enough that Stannoth could see the huge-but-bloodless gash across his throat. Stannoth assumed that it was a parting gift from the Nightshade.

It was (thankfully) the only thing he was wrong about.

"Your own... your people... Don't understand..."

"O' course ye don't. Nobody dae. Nobody but meself, nobody but me an' 'er. It just dunna matter tae ye. I cannae even feed ye tae 'er. Yer never even gonna see 'er, ye ain't worthy. Neither was yer bitch. Suncursed bastards! Nae worthy tae look through yer metal eyes at th' sun, an' sure be it all ye ain't worthy tae look at *'er* blessed beauty!" he screamed.

"Killed children? Killed... your own kind?" Stannoth managed to croak out.

The dwarf nodded with a manic glee. "Sh's hungry. Lost, lost fer so long. Found 'er. Miners makin' a new pass off towards th' Equallin' Mountains, puttin' down th' glowin' crystals fer us tae see by as we get lower and deeper an' all that. Wanted tae build a tunnel tae 'em. They found 'er, lost, trapped in a broken cave. Sh's been in there, in there fer so long. An' with those undyin' freaks! Sh' couldn't take 'em. Tried fer so many years, decades, centuries? Time, tae much time."

"You won't... they'll kill you..."

"They cannae kill me! Sh' made me more than alive! They cannae, ye cannae, nobody cannae! Ye cannae kill *death*, ye blind lil' fisker!" he said with a rancorous laugh. The golem squeezed again on Stannoth's throat. He got one last pained moan out as he started to feel the world swim around him. If it didn't let go...

"This critter? One o' mine. Used it tae kill th' blind bitch. Only fittin' tae use it tae put ye down intae th' ground right with 'er."

That he used the golem as a murder weapon wasn't much of a surprise. Still, it gave Stannoth an opening that Vestalic could have never seen coming. While the dwarf cackled in his golden armor, he stopped struggling and sagged limply into the construct's grip. It picked him up and then shoved him back against the wall for a third time, crushing him against the cold brick. It shook him like a rag doll while the geomancer continued to watch with undisguised, twisted glee. He kept the ruse up through the agonizing pain for nearly a complete minute before making his play.

Stannoth tried to challenge him around the crushing hand on his throat "Killed her, not me," he snarled. What actually came out was an unintelligible gasp, but he really did try to snarl it. Nobody's perfect.

Less than a moment later, he freed a stone of his own out of one of the hidden pockets in his cloak and jammed it into the middle of the construct. Vestalic didn't see him do it. The golem did, but didn't know how to react... or even if it should.

It was living rock. Stones weren't normally thought to be blessed with wisdom. It wasn't part of their nature; they were rocks.

It really couldn't have done anything anyway. A heartbeat later the crystal bomb blew forward and reduced half of the largest stones to a hundred shards that rained down on the geomancer — and with a flash of dark violet light, a second explosion ripped into the gut of the golem. The sound from it was indescribable. How does stone scream? How can it scream?

Loudly, apparently, and violently.

Chunks of rock tore into his armor like they were launched by a ballista. A few penetrated, but not many, and not deeply. Stone flew in every direction as the damian fell to the floor. The impact blew the midriff of the construct apart, splitting it in half. As bits of stone drew blood on the geomancer's face, he quit laughing... not that it mattered what *he* did anymore.

There was a rule. One very, very important rule. If you kill a necromancer? You need to make *damn* sure that the spirit goes along with the body.

Stannoth slammed his hands down on top of the journal. A wave of magic rippled from the impact and tore a hole between the worlds, just long enough, just large enough, to give birth to nothing but raw rage. With the right spells to bring them back, those that can control the dead always seem to be chronically *pissed*.

With a terrifying scream, Lessiana's anger was made manifest. Nearly transparent, the soul of the fallen damian pulled herself into the world and flew through the air to her murderer. The huntsman smiled victoriously. The geomancer... didn't.

Vestalic managed to voice a choked scream before her spirit barreled into him. Nude but for a cloak over her back, she had been twice his height in life. In death? Her hate given form, her body swelled to double that. If it had just been a physical fight between the pair, it would have been just short of impossible even on his best day.

In a spiritual one? His ability to defend himself in that kind of fight was far weaker than his ability to live through mortal wounds (and she gave him no shortage of new ones to wear with dishonor). With fingernails as strong as diamonds and teeth turned into little more than razor blades, the spirit ripped skin from his bones and threw him past the sand-stuffed corpse in the doorway and out of the nursery.

What she did out there was between her and him, and it didn't sound... fun. Stannoth started to join their party, but the golem wasn't done with him yet. Or rather, it was, but the thing that had been merged with it wasn't. Grains of sand coalesced in the air in the middle of the room while he watched.

It manifested quickly. No, not an it, a she. A woman - no, a poorly-crafted caricature of one - suddenly stood in the middle of the room. Sand continued to ripple over her like waves of water, and Stannoth could tell that she had seen far better days. Her face kept sagging down to her neck before reforming again and again.

One leg had a hole that he could see through. She had one ornate, angelic wing that looked like it might let her take flight, but the other the other was little more than a sandy stump. She didn't seem to need either of them to float over the ground. There were marks and wounds all over her, things that should have vanished as the sand flowed over and through them.

They didn't. They persisted no matter how hard she struggled to force them closed. There was something in her face that he somehow recognized. It radiated off of her. She was in pain. She was in so much pain. This must be the creature that Vestalic had found, his 'lady.'

She locked her gaze on the damian, and then turned her head to look outside to the screaming dwarf. She wavered as Stannoth pulled a knife out of its sheath. *"Made him like me. He undying now. Do what I can't do. Do for God. He do. I can't. He do what God say do. God say harvest. Can't harvest. He harvest."* The woman reached into her chest and pulled out a ruby, glowing faintly through the sand. She gave it a final longing look, then sadly dropped her eyes to the floor. *"Now he broken like me. He can't harvest no more. He... he like me."* With a sobbing cry, she collapsed in upon herself and melted away into cracks in the floor before the huntsman could try to do anything with her at all.

Out in the hallway, the screaming had stopped, and Lessiana's spirit was gone. Laying in a bloody heap on the floor, the dwarf was grateful for her departure. But only for a moment. The hunter staggered out of the ruined nursery and looked down at the geomancer with the same kind of cold delight a cat gives a mouse. "Undying?" Stannoth asked out-loud, debating if he should question the little bastard or put him through a test.

With a growl that sent pain radiating from his battered throat, he thrust an arrow like a dagger into Vestalic's left eye and out the back of his head hard enough to chip the head on the stone floor. The dwarf screamed in raw agony... and didn't stop, even after the hunter twisted the wooden spike and forth again, and again, and again. When the spellcaster didn't stop screaming, he had his answer.

Vestalic passed the test.

He was apparently immortal.

Unfortunately for him.

Elrok watched as the other reavers turned and ran away in all directions. The man in the red robe flexed his hand and shook the last vestiges of the one he had killed into the sand. They vanished as quickly as they fell, swallowed by time eternal. "Funny creatures, those. They gain nothing from rending souls but they are compelled to do so. They do not eat, and they do not breed, but yet, they are compelled. Divine will pressed upon them by their Creator." He looked up at the dwarf and smiled. "Whom, I may add, is an ass of a Godling. Absolutely no class, no decorum, at all. Even worse, He's a bore to speak to. I would not recommend it."

The dwarf didn't know where to begin. "Killed it? Ye... killed it? So easy? Ain't supposed tae be a thin' in th' veil that canna hurt... nae whatever that critter was, nae a mort...? Nae anythin' killin' anythin'?" he marveled, in no small part bewildered.

He smiled, letting the question slide. "Funny creatures, your kind as well. They have been keeping me company lately."

Elrok looked past him, behind him, and saw them. There were easily twenty, if not more; the only blessing was that he didn't see any of the children. None of them said a word. Or smiled. Or reacted. They just stood there, dressed in whatever garb they had worn upon their death, in a loose pack, and watched. "Me kin..."

"You have, well, I suppose *they* have, always intrigued me. Your people. Always so willing to fight. Always willing to be the masters of your own fate. Fight to the last breath for what you have taken as your own." He tossed the dwarf an annoyed glare. Cold red eyes, darker than his robe, framed by his dusky skin were absolutely dim with disgust. "Absolutely irritating beyond all measure for any of the rest of us to listen to you *talk*... but, you are intriguing."

"Their souls. Ye've trapped them... who are ye, what are ye?" he demanded.

"No, not imprisoned. As I said – they simply intrigue me. I have other things to do at the moment than hold them back from their next life. Truthfully, they were simply here when I came to look around. They should not be. Neither should *you*. It left me curious. So. I have stayed with them. Just... to see. It is not me that has bound them here. This is their own desire. It is an odd wish, but it is theirs alone."

Shaking his head in confusion, he looked around and tried to make sense out of anything around him. Anything at all. The sky, the sands, the landscape nearly unbroken in every direction except for the farthest reaches where a mountain could be seen stretching to the sky. Or behind him, as the land vanished into thickening fog. "This ain't th' veil... where am I? Where did ye pull me? An' who in th' pits *are* ye tae be able tae keep me people here?"

The man in the red robe clicked his tongue, scolding him. "As I said. I have not done a thing to them. We talked. Some. They are not the most chatty. Of course, I doubt I would be either. *She* truly did a number one every single one of them. Honestly. I am impressed they were able to hang on this close to the living world after that. You do have to give it to the poor thing. Her work is as thorough as it is inspired."

"Sh' who? An iffin' ye ain't 'ere tae hurt 'em... who are ye? Tell me, demon, who are ye?"

The man scowled a little deeper. "I am no demon, to begin with. I have not insulted *you* so I ask that you be so kind as to not insult *me*. I am not the one you need to worry about. I am just an observer. Nothing but luck for us both to be so fortunate to meet each other. Your manners be damned, of course." He waited for a second while Elrok tried to digest the remarks. "But. You are just a dwarf, so I know not to expect much from you in the way of culture. You could at least *pretend*, for the sake of things. Could you not?"

"Ye ain't makin' any damned kindae sense. I dunna have any kinda damned clue who ye are or how I ended up 'ere. And ye talk tae damn much without givin' me a single damned answer."

"Oh dwarfie. Came here to find answers and all you do is ask the wrong questions. Who I am is not important for you. She, as I have said so often, is. She is a very *big* problem for you."

"WHO? Ye talk in riddles!"

"Well. We tend to dispense with the... classifications, I suppose, that is the closest word for it... that your kind uses. We simply call them collectors. You... Well. What do you call a creature made by a God of unique drive, built within their image? One that exists for a single minded-purpose, not seen outside of their home realm?"

A sudden, horrible feeling landed in the dwarf's stomach. "Nae. Ye mean... an elemental."

"Yes, there you go. See? I knew you could do this. And what kind of elemental might cause all of this grief? One that could move through barriers physical and magical with relative ease, one that could strike silently, and one that can claim a soul with a simple touch? Given the nature of your problem, I am a little disappointed that you have not yet been able to place a name to it." He paused for a breath and then shook his head. "Simply unfathomable."

That feeling took a new life in a hurry (an ironic statement, given its exact nature). "An elemental of death. Nae. Ye canna be sayin' that someone 'as summoned a bleedin' death elemental..."

"Yes, I can. I am. A little lost reaper, trapped between beauty and duty, purpose and failure. She is adorable, if not completely mad. Yes, I do mean completely. We do mad in these parts quite often, so I assure you, we are something of experts on the condition. Lost her mind; too many years in the dark, too many things she is to do, but she cannot. I really do not envy her her fate," then slowly a little light began to gleam in his eyes. "You know, it almost reeks of home."

That cold feeling only got worse. "Quite th' tale. An' who are ye tae be trusted?"

The stranger tossed his head back and laughed out loud. The dwarves behind him backed away almost as a unit. Elrok shared their trepidation. "TRUSTED? Oh you funny little man! There is no trust to be had here. You are not paying *any* kind of attention, are you? Did you not see on which side of the veil you fell? Not only are you not where you should be, you are in the next-to-last place you would *want* to be. Truly; that is not a play on words. You are *in* the *next-to-last place!* It only gets worse from here, but no, you are not smart enough to piece it together."

"I know me spellwork. I'ma only 'ere tae see, not tae touch. Th' rules o' th' magic say I cannae die 'ere... that there's nae a way fer any o' th' things that flitter in th' veil tae touch me..."

"You really believe that? Oh, the *rules*. The only ones that care about the rules are the Gods. Do you see any Gods here, little man? Do you think those reavers care about your vaunted *rules*? No, of course they do not. They have Their own. Even if you think that Their rules are less than valid does not mean that *They* think so. Or that I do. Or that anyone else does. Perception does not always make an accurate reality. What is it that *you* see that makes *you* think that *your* views of the world matters more than what anyone else practices?"

"I see me kin," he defiantly snapped back. "An' I see a blowhard that's got nae right tae keep me from findin' a way tae help me people get tae where they should be, an' not be trapped 'ere with ye... whomever ye are... wherever this blasted place is..."

"Oh little dwarfie. I have every right to keep you here. You are not where you should be. Not where *any* of the 'living' should be. Not where you meant to be. You are in my home."

Elrok took a nervous gulp of air (even if there was no air present to gulp). "Yer... yer home?"

The man in the red looked around for a long moment before answering. "Well, no. My yard, really. Or at least, my neighborhood. Either way, what happens to you next is *entirely* my decision." He watched the lost huntsman start to back away, then pointed at something behind him. "I do have some measure of dominion here. Do recognize that."

Elrok spared a glance back. He immediately wished he hadn't. A bank of cinder-colored clouds had appeared where nothing had been before. A single crack of thunder-less lightning flashed within the storm. "Blessed be, what is that...?"

The observer allowed a faint smile on his dark face to assure the dwarf that *his* lack of fear was something that he should be gravely concerned over. "I would not get too far in that direction, little man, because then you *will* be in my home. I do not believe you would want that."

Desperately, the dwarf tried to think of a way to make a weapon, use a weapon, use something to try and get away. "Ye've nae right... none, nae man has a right tae keep me 'ere, or them, or..."

"I said that I was not a demon. I did not say that I was a mere man. I am, however, taking a shine to you. You are an interesting one, if not in need of an education. Do your people not have schools? People to teach you the most basic of protocols?"

He was getting royally tired of being talked down to. "I'm nae o' th' opinion that's such a good thin'... an' I save me manners fer those that I know are worth 'em."

There was a short cackle of echoing laughter. "Oh, little man, you have *no* idea of what I am worth to you. As for the other? I did not say that my interest in you was a good thing, did I?"

Elrok nervously swallowed. Then he realized that he shouldn't have been able to do that. Not in the veil. It was a little thing, a simple thing, but it put all of this into terrifying perspective. "Nae good fer whom?"

"For us both. Maybe it is. Maybe not. Remember this though: I lied. Gods do not care about 'rules'. Gods do not care about little men or little dwarves. Gods are bored and spiteful things. When time is eternal the only reason They bothered to make you is to entertain themselves. You are just there for Them to play with. To see what makes things go light and dark. To automatically, naturally sort out what They are too disinterested to bother with Themselves. So tell me, little dwarfie, why do you think anything on this side of eternity cares about what you, in your tiny, short-lived, insignificant mind, *thinks?*"

Elrok looked at him and squared his shoulders. If this yammering bastard was going to be insulting, he was too. "I suppose that's th' easiest thin' I canna say."

"Amuse me then, little dwarfie," the other man challenged with a smirk. "What *is* your answer?"

"Because, one day, it'll be me back 'ere, wherever this 'ere is, in these sands, lookin' in, lookin' down, lookin' back, an ye'll be one o' th' first people-thins' I'll be a commin' tae talk tae. An' things'll be a tad different then."

With another peal of laughter, the man in the red robe shook his head. "Oh! Little dwarfie, not so little, are you? I am a 'people-thing,' am I? That is almost endearing. Well. When you do, when we meet again, we will make a point to sit down and chat once more. I think you and I will be great friends then. One day." He looked at the dwarf and ran a finger over his lips. "Or... or I will simply eat you. Never know in this day and age, honestly."

"Momma always said that friends are worth makin'," the dwarf sarcastically shot back. "An' I dunnae go down nae tae easily, so whatever ye are, dunnae go thinkin' I'd taste nae tae good slidin' down yer gullet."

"A wise woman. And I would not dream of it without proper seasoning." He looked back at the sand at his feet and frowned. No, he looked *through* the sand at something completely different and growled under his breath. "Oh that idiot is going to get himself killed," he sighed. "And me, engaged with a pebble-brained small-minded mercenary! Oh, damn it. I no longer have time for this."

"An' who is it ye be talkin' about now? Th' boy? Stanny?"

After a moment's concentration, the observer shook his head. "No. My idiot. Not yours. Your idiot is doing well enough on his own. Although... well. He could be doing better, I suppose. He is assuredly going to feel that hammering in the morning - if he makes it that long."

"More doubletalk. Can ye nae say a damned thin' that makes sense? Who is yer idiot? Another damned demon down in th' tunnels?"

"No, my idiot is in the scrubs above your tunnels. He really *is* an idiot; I have absolutely no idea what our father was thinking. He could have picked any other woman to bed. I know willing pit-hounds who would have squeezed something out that would be bigger, stronger, and covered in scales and horns that would be *far* easier to deal with than this one-eyed moron he saddled me with. Paladins! Is there no limit to the depths of their stupidity? It as is if blind obedience to the Heavens requires them to give up their sense of... reason!"

Elrok tried to figure out who this stranger could have possibly meant, and then asked.

With an annoyed glare, the observer brushed him off. "Oh. He is nobody that *you* of all people need to worry about." Then he sighed, again, and looked back down at... whomever 'his' idiot was. "Well. This is amusing, but you and I both have other and better things to do. *Your* idiot is somehow as interesting as you are, if you could believe it. Entirely different reasons, but yes, he is as interesting as you are. I suppose I will have to keep a watch on him, too. Ugh. Just ugh. Do you have *any* idea how much effort it takes to get a decent pair of eyes on interesting people? It is an absolute drain."

"Me idiot? Fanim?"

"No. The other one. The useful one. The one with the metal eyes."

"That one be nae friend o' mine."

"No. Of course not. Too much said and done between your people.

Well. Not your friend today. He will be though. Plain as all day; you two are far too much alike for anything else to come of it. There are many things that you are and will be – and wrong will frequently be one of them. You *are* a... oh, what is it they call your kind? Tunnel-rats? Yes, that is it. You are just a tunnel-rat, after all. Your prey is too, but not entirely."

"Ye know what it is. Ye know, an' yer just standin' 'ere, an' ye still won't say a damned thin' I cannae actually *use* fer this bleedin' mess! Fer all I know, yer idiot is th' cause o' *me* trouble! Let alone who it is ye really are!"

The man in the red robe quit trying to hide his scorn. "My idiot is *not* causing your problem. He is dealing with a facet of it, yes, but it is not yours. I do not want you involving yourself in his problem – *my* problem – although I imagine you will try." He straightened himself up and *pulled* power to him, making the sands around his feet billow up into the air all around his legs. "Do not."

"An' should I be afraid that ye can make this sand move? A swift breeze canna dae th' same."

"Since you will not drop it otherwise, just know I am a messenger of Someone long-suffering and much more important in the grand scheme of things than you will ever be, and He has far less patience for a resolution of all of these little squabbles seemingly popping in and out of thin air than you could possibly believe."

"An'...? Me problem? There's nae a class out there tae teach a man how tae kill death! Let alone how tae solve th' fate o' me people stuck 'ere!"

"Your people? You truly care about them? Their well being? Interesting. You are afraid of where you are... but you would stop to argue over their fate instead of trying to find a way to leave? Hmm. Odd. You do intrigue me."

"O' *course* I care about 'em! That's why I came so damned far 'ere, havin' tae put up with th' same type o' fiskers that got me sister killed, that threatened to 'ave me family murdered iffin' I didn't give up me claim tae th' throne! I'd nae have bothered tae make it all this damned far an' all iffin' I didn't *care* about 'em! I'ma even off an' workin' with a damned *damian* tae dae it, tae boot!"

With a soft 'huh' of surprise, his host digested his little outburst. "Fair is fair. You move me with your passion. Well. I do have dominion here, so... well. Hmm. Well... okay. When my idiot is through being an idiot, or at least takes a breather from one act of stupidity before his next, I will see to it that they all go the places that they should go and do not get stuck in this otherwise eternal expanse. It would be a far too dull fate for a people as oddly entertaining as yours are."

Elrok heard it — but barely believed it. "An'... an' iffin' yer willin' tae dae that fer 'em, what about th' elemental? Th' one ye said was trapped between beauty an' duty? Iffin' ye've got so much power tae be able tae say ye've got dominion 'ere o' all places, surely ye can..."

"I can do many things. Do not push your luck or the limits of my kindness. I am already going well out of my way to do things for you." He shook his head. "You see so much, yet you do not understand a word I have said. Bear witness, little man, to what I do, and what I say. She is like these sands — eternal. But sand is not always sand." He looked into his hand and plucked a chunk of the blackened reaver's corpse from it, before crushing it into a fine powder that trickled onto the ground.

"Bear witness? Tae what?"

"What you have seen. Remember that, or do not." He sighed and glanced at him again. "She will kill you, or she will not. The choice is yours."

Then, with a flick of his hand, Elrok felt a wave of power hit him across his stomach before the world started to swim in his vision. The cold feeling began to fade and the sand started to feel more solid under his feet even as the world around him started to vanish into nothing. His choked-off cry of pain had barely faded when he heard the man's voice again.

"OH! And dwarfie? The next time you travel to the ether, you had best make sure that someone does not come around and *change your spell* before you cast it! You never know who you might end up meeting... and I will *not* be here to save your tiny little soul the next time!"

As the world came into focus, the freaked-out dwarf groggily opened his eyes. It took a few long silent moments before he was able to make sense of the palpable anger coming from the others in the room, not to mention why so many had crossbows, swords, and maces held tightly in their hands. Or why they all looked like they were terrified that the world was about to end at any given moment. Or why Fanim stood at the chapel entrance with blisteringly-hot rocks spinning in the air between his hands, much like the inside of a raging volcano.

Stannoth was there, as was Bayetta, and six other dwarven guards. Everyone was looking at a quivering lump on the ground, covered with a thick canvas sack. The lump had his partner's knee square on the center of it, and he had his axe out and pressed into the sheet. "Welcome back," the damian finally said. "Was concerned."

"Out 'an out bloody worried, ye mean," Bayetta muttered.

"Yes."

Elrok tried to shake his head again. "Tha... thank ye," he mumbled. "What... who's... under th' blanket?"

"Something of yours."

"O' mine?"

"Yes."

"An' what would ye... nae, wait, need tae dae somethin' first," he muttered, slowly standing up, looking much the worse the wear. Without another word or warning, he staggered over to the Gemwarden, and drove his fist into Fanim's mouth. The elder dwarf fell, spitting blood in an arc as he went. The stones he had held in the air went flying everywhere, hitting one guard while the others ducked out of the way.

Fanim sputtered in shock and tried to say something between broken teeth. Elrok didn't seem to have the desire to give him a chance to ask why, and rocked his head back against the ground with another heartfelt punch. "Ye fiskin' *idiot*. Cannae blame all this mess on ye, but I be damned sure ye ain't bright enough tae help tae *fix* it!"

"Ye outta o' yer damned mind?!" he managed to shout back, struggling to back away from the attack. "I did everythin' in me power tae try tae save lives!"

"Th' fiskin' pits ye did," Elrok seethed. "Stanny! Boy! Ye said ye were havin' a wee bit o' trouble seein' all th' things down 'ere, aye?"

The damian was enjoying the show far too much to want to interrupt (even with the squirming mass under his knee). But after Elrok repeated himself a second time, he acknowledged it. "Yes. Since arrival."

It was all that his companion needed. "Ye. Ye activated a spell. Somethin' tae block their sight. Left it on while 'is kin was 'ere, tryin' tae help ye, an' ye let 'er get killed because o' it. Left it on, didn't think tae maybe take it off when ye saw that one o' yer own was workin' with him. Fiskin' with people tryin' tae *save* yer worthless ass!"

"HELP? Help from WHO? For all we knew they *were* th' ones doin' it! Ye think we'd risk makin' life easier fer 'em? Fools were blinded fer a reason. An' tried tae take th' tunnels from us," the Gemwarden snarled. "Dunnae ye remember what they did tae us? Tae yer own?"

Invoking that memory only made the dwarf with the flattened nose even angrier. He shoved a guard away that was trying, ineffectively, to pry him away from their stone-encrusted leader. With a snarl, he stopped down – *hard* – on Fanim's leg, eliciting a satisfying crack and scream. The sound made Stannoth smile while everyone else cringed.

Yet, nobody else seemed to be in such a hurry to pry the shorter hunter off of him. "Dunnae ye *dare*. I watched, *watched* me uncle an' 'is vapid woman, an' me sis, all three o' 'em, get yanked tae th' shadows, an' get butchered by 'is kin an' those that let 'em!" he shouted, pointing back at the damian. "An' yet! Yet, I'ma still willin' tae be 'ere, right 'ere, with 'im tae save yer old racist wrinkled ass, ye little SHIT!"

"An' if they'd dae that tae *yer* own, what makes ye think they'd nae dae it 'ere? Wouldn't try tae take our homes from all o' us?!"

"Take *what*? What is it ye have 'ere that's worth all this bloodshed?" Elrok shouted, looking back and forth between Fanim, Bayetta, the lump, and the guards. "That's th' thin' I just cannae figure. There's a critter loose, causin' pain, needs tae die. Aye. Surely. Makes nae shortage o' sense that it needs tae be ripped apart. But ye," he ranted, pointing over at Bayetta, "ye, said ye asked fer us. Personally."

She slowly nodded at him, suddenly looking uncomfortable for all the world.

"An' Talonbur. That fisker said we've been tasked 'ere by Aidenchal. Right, Stanny?"

The archer tilted his head slightly. And replied with a simple "Yes," intrigued by the fresh line of questions.

"So. Help me tae get a grip on all o' this. Th' humans are topside, fightin' an' somethin' stupid, as they all want tae dae. An' iffin' I'ma seein' an' hearin' things right, they've got a really bloody mess goin' on. This awfulness down 'ere, it ain't completely related tae it. But, it's got a lot o' potential tae make th' mess topside worse. Stanny, ye figure out what that stuffs might be?"

"Yes. War-tribes. Immortals."

Elrok moved away from Fanim, rubbing at his jaw while he thought it through. "Immortals? Well now. Sounds familiar. Our boy in th' pit?"

The damian gave a nod of us own.

With a scowl, Elrok looked back and forth between the Gemwarden and the girl that had 'hired' them. "So. It ain't th' fact that th' warren is bein' attacked that's th' problem. It's that what's been doin' th' killin' is interferin' with whatever Aidenchal is off an' doin' up under th' sun." The disgust on his face spoke volumes. "Yer tae busy tryin' tae convince us that yer tae be trusted tae be o' any use tae us," he said as he pointed at her, before turning and making a gesture with his middle finger at the leader of the warren. "An' yer tae damn busy tryin' tae make up fer old sins tae quickly get an end tae any kinda bloodshed!"

"Gold makes liars," Stannoth mused. "Can't trust the clients. Could leave."

The dwarf turned his foul gaze over at him. For a change, the taller hunter decided it was best to stop now while he was ahead. "We *ain't* leavin' until th' job is done, an' we get ourselves our gold. Cannae believe a word that either o' these tae idiots breathe out, but th' dead want answers, even if *we* ain't gonna be getting' any."

That made the archer smile all over again. "Asking the wrong people."

"Oh? An' ye've got someone under th' tarp that can put a better spin on all o' this right bloody fiskered mess?"

"Yes. Something of yours."

"Ye said that already. Yer mother ever tell ye tae tease a hungry man is a pisser o' a sin? Just had enough o' that shit tae last me a damned lifetime. Or a trio o' 'em back tae back."

The other hunter pulled the bag back, and spat on the captive's face in an uncharacteristic display of emotion. Elrok looked confused as he looked at the Geomancer, nude from the waist up. The gash in his throat was wide open for everyone to see, as were the rough wounds that *both* damians had inflicted through the fight. "Of yours," he repeated.

"Erm. Canna ye dae me a favor an' help me out a lil' more? Dae I know 'im?"

Fanim cleared up the confusion. "Me pupil. Trained 'im since 'e could pick up a rock. An', nae, Stannoth ain't th' one tae do all th' damage on 'im. Bastard has been behind it, all o' it, an' it looks like th' other damian had went an' did some pain before sh' lost 'er life. Vestalic has been doin' more than we ever coulda guessed anyone was," he begrudgingly muttered, spitting out bits of a bloody tooth as he stood back up. Pain shot through his leg and left a shine in his aura that Stannoth openly smiled about.

He was right and wrong — but even knowing better, the damian decided to let the part about the 'new player' in Lessiana's journal. He was quickly beginning to (grudgingly) trust Elrok, but the others? Not a chance. If someone wanted to try and rip Vestalic's head off, that meant they might have an ally... whomever, or wherever, she was. "Been feeding a 'fallen angel.' He dies. It starves. We're done."

That part, at least, he had to share.

The dwarf shook his head as he shambled over to them. Every inch of his body hurt and he felt like he had been buried in a snowdrift for a week without food or water. Sweat had soaked through all of his clothes, and the taste of bile was on the back of his tongue. "We've... other problems, bigger problems, 'cause it ain't an angel. Nae. An angel we could dae somethin..." he started, then turned and quickly looked at the marks he had drawn on the floor. "Unbe... fisk me, oh just fisk me..."

"Underprince?" Fanim asked, concern covering his face as he looked at the shape his friend was in.

"Fiskin'... this, this ain't what I wrote... unbelievable... 'e couldn't've known this..."

"Elrok?" It was Bayetta this time.

"We've a bigger problem. Elemental. Dead one."

"Dead? Just saw it. Barely an hour back," Stannoth disputed. "You kill it? In the veil? How?"

"Death, death, nae dead. Elemantalkin... Death. Sorry, I'ma..."

The damian's face shot up to look at his companion. "You know this how?"

As blood slowly drained from his face, Elrok struggled to reply. "Found... answers. An' me kin. Ye were right — lots o' thins out there. Shit that shouldn't be. Lookin' in at us. Waitin' fer us. Reavers, this elemental, other critters, tae. Bad... it's bad, it's all *bad* in there. An' 'e... 'e changed me spell... Bad where 'e sent me..."

Stannoth stared intently at him and started to blanch. "Not into the veil."

"Nae... nae, not intae th' veil." He hands shook as the full realization of how close he had really been to being lost forever under the sands. "Someplace a bit past that."

"Bury this? Then track the elemental?" his partner asked, squeezing Vestalic's throat while rolling violent, unpleasant thoughts through his mind.

Elrok stared down at the should-be-mortal wounds that covered Vestalic. "Let us have a wee bit o' a chat with 'im, an' see what 'e says an' all. Always did hear yer folk were good at that kinda thin'. Any truth tae that?"

It was for the best for everyone in the room that he was hard to read on a good day. "Can you dig?"

Today was not good day.

The only woman with them cleared her throat. "'e's killed a lot o' us. An' yer kin, an' yer fellows. Cannae just kill 'im, canna just bury 'im. 'e's gotta face some kindae justice."

"He will," Stannoth assured her. "Elrok?"

"Aye?"

"I'll ask. You dig." he said as he pressed his axe back into Vestalic's empty eye. The Geomancer tried to howl through the mud that Fanim had filled his mouth with, all-the-while thrashing on the floor, trying to get away. His dwarven companion gave a silent nod of his head for an answer.

One to dig, one to see. It was a good arrangement for everyone.

Except for Vestalic.

IV. TO REAP A REAPER

It was difficult to tell time underground. Without a sun to guide you, concepts like 'day' and night' are difficult at best to manage. At worst, it was near impossible. The dwarves and the damians had both figured out a way to keep track of the time (and not rely on silly measures like 'candlemarks').

Long ago, the little ones discovered a small crystal that grew in some of the caves closer to the overland that, as the day went by, would change colors. When it was a soft gold, it was day. At night, it shifted to a soft silver. After years of experimenting, they had even discovered how to grow them. This resulted in pathways from one warren to another being illuminated with the glowing stones – a marvel of magic and engineering. Never again would any cave be too dark, and no unwanted night would ever creep into their homes. They could even break pieces off and carry them in their pockets.

Or even make jewelry from them, as some had done. Elrok didn't care for the jewelry or for the gaudy look on his clothes, but he did carry one with him in his belt at all times. What he failed to realize was that that one stone, that one simple crystal? That was one of the most valuable things that the Blackstone Trading Company had ever discovered. Humans didn't have access to anything even remotely like it without having to dig up significant piles of gold to be shoveled to the overpriced Granalchi (the irony being that they needed light in those very caves to do that).

As luck would have it, Kepershal was where that light had first been discovered, ages ago. As it grew into the other parts of the Crystal Kingdom through adventures in geomancy, the need to protect the glowing birthplace of the light faded until it was barely a memory. Once it was everywhere, why would it matter? (Unless, of course, you needed access to the original stones to figure out how to craft them yourself.)

In many ways, it was exactly why Master Aidenchal wanted the warren to be cleansed. Fanim didn't know it, and Bayetta could only guess. If you could grow light, the shadows would always be at your mercy, and nobody would be forced to suffer the stench of smoking flames or to deal with a temperamental sun. A feat of enchanted engineering that would remove the need to rely on mages for underground projects? To light every road? Any path? No home would ever be dark. No city at risk of things lurking in the shadows.

Yes, the light – and the location – were two things that Blackstone wanted. Not just badly, but very badly. The elemental was in the way (their other problems overhead notwithstanding). Stannoth and Elrok would solve the problem where others before them had failed, or...

...or, Aidenchal would send an army into the warren, and another, and another, until the cause of it was either dead or too bloated from gorging itself on their dead bodies to matter. Of course that meant that the warren wouldn't be there any longer and *that* would cause some long-term problems with the rest of the Crystal Kingdom. But, he really didn't care. Just as long as it was solved, he didn't *care*.

Of course, neither Stannoth nor Elrok had any way to know any of this. The BeaST played their cards close to the chest. It was the only way *to* play. And in matters of equal fact, the damians once again were nowhere near as lucky as their smug neighbors. Equal, yet opposite, and where the dwarves had a resource that made their lives easy and that was lusted after by the other races of men...

Stannoth grunted unhappily. The dwarf had taken the first watch, and that damn gem was just magical enough to make the ether vibrate all night. What might be ignored during waking hours, became almost unbearably annoying when trying to sleep. He had (finally) ruled out out choking Elrok to death with it. But it had taken him hours to come to that conclusion.

When the little bastard finally woke up the next morning, he asked where that gem was. When Stannoth pulled shattered (yet unfortunately still glowing) bits of it out of the bag behind him, the dwarf blinked a few times and asked him how he knew what time it was if he hadn't been looking at the rock.

To which, a reply of "The ether," was met with a dumb stare. Condemned to the dark, even the youngest of their kind could see the constant currents of the ether in the world between worlds. Over the course of the day, it ebbed and flowed, much like the tide. It was there for anyone to see, but most couldn't. As such, it had all the value in the world to the suncursed.

But again, absolutely no value to anyone else.

And he still wanted to choke the dwarf with his ugly little rock even hours after they broke camp and left the warren. The line of conversation wasn't helping much either. "I cannae believe that 'e would dae such a thin'," Elrok exclaimed for the tenth time in half as many hours. "How? How dae ye... dae that? Tae yer own people?"

"Love. Makes men mad."

"Madness is one thin'," the dwarf countered. "But 'e aligned 'imself with it. An' tae what possible end? Blamin' th' people o' th' War God fer this stupid elemental tae get trapped down 'ere? Killin' women, killin' children, tae drive th' rest o' th' warren away? Wantin' tae use it as a base fer 'is own private war?"

Stannoth shook his head. "Revenge."

"Oh I get revenge. I'ma thinkin' we both dae. But this?"

"His woman went mad. You'd aid yours"

The dwarf spit on the ground. "*Me* wife would never *be* mad. Sh' *makes* men mad. An' that thin' is nae wife. It's a bloody force o' nature. All it is. Ain't nothin' more than that. Just a force, ye know? Most natural one o' 'em all. Ye cannae love a force o' nature."

He gave it a couple minutes of thought before he answered. "Niamiss's followers do."

"O' *course* they dae. Th' bitch *is* Love. An' it'll be somethin' o' a pleasant day in th' Abyss before either o' us ever meet one o' 'em that's any kinda sane. *An'* none o' '*em* 'ave *ever* wanted tae murder people an' build an army o' stone tae attack th' over-realms tae win 'er favor." He grumbled something impolite under his breath and shook his head. "Fiskin' madness, boy, fiskin' madness."

With a silent nod, the damian agreed. That really had been Vestalic's plan all along. In his duties as the warren's apprentice Geomancer, he had found a sealed cavern and made the mistake of

76

opening it. He had been met almost immediately by the maddened, undying hulks that the elemental had been desperately trying to kill for centuries.

The men with him had been killed outright, and little was left of their bodies. When the wretched creatures turned to him, he was able to work his magic to quickly re-entomb the room – but his stonework was imperfect, and cracks were left in it. The elemental pushed through those cracks and filled him. It came through so slowly that its magic didn't kill him outright; instead, it infused his every pore. She was made of sand eternal and coupled with his magical affinity with all-things rock, it did something that neither could have expected.

As his essence was filled with her, his sanity cracked. He felt her pain and felt her loss and felt her own insanity, brought upon by centuries of attempting to kill men that by divine edict, could not die. And her duty was equally as divinely driven; her very purpose was to reap souls that otherwise would not pass on their own. Her essence was trapped in an unending loop away from her creator and outside of the guidance or care of theirs.

As the Geomancer's mental focus collapsed, he gained pity for the creature. Pity soon turned to love and then obsession. Growing from that, a desire to feed her so as to help return her own mind blossomed. Then afterwards, rage, anger, hate. All of that and so much more, aimed at the God of War. The dwarves were a means to an end, nothing more, nothing less. First as 'food,' then as a place to build his own army of dust, crystal, and stone.

"An' I swear I cannae understand what in th' world 'e planned tae dae after 'e raised 'is army. Go tae war with War?"

"Doubt he even knew," Stannoth grumbled.

There was just one nagging question – would letting her kill bring her some kind of peace? The hunters doubted it. Dredging a river wouldn't calm it - it merely let the current flow deeper, let it do what the waters needed to do. They weren't able to get any kind of evidence that his methods had been working. He *believed* that it did, though though neither thought he was right - just obsessed.

He willingly offered a home for the elemental in his own body. It, in turn, left enough of itself for him to otherwise live a very long life – very, very long, and near immortal. Not *invulnerable*, as he found out, but practically immortal. Vestalic realized after the bulk of his kin ran away from the warrens that he needed to recover strength from his fight with Lessiana before he could challenge Fanim for control of the tunnels.

He had been hidden away doing just that when Stannoth and Elrok arrived at the quarry. Nobody paid another refugee any mind, and why would they? He had a scarf around his throat and claimed that he had gotten scratched by some tunnel-crawling bug. It had just enough of a glimmer of truth to ensure that nobody would question his story, let alone the hunters when they had arrived topside

They considered themselves blessed by the Goddess of Luck for him to be so far gone that he never considered burying them alive when he sent them through the stone and into the warrens. He had wanted to entomb the Nightshade, but he didn't think he could explain away her disappearance to the rest of the warren. He also assumed that whoever had sent for them would soon wonder where they went.

If he hadn't...

They didn't want to contemplate the 'what if.'

The Geomancer regretted his decision to let the hunters live almost immediately. His attack on Stannoth was rushed and panicked; nobody had realized he had even returned to the warren. If he had been discovered before he could strike, it would have been over before it started.

He (correctly) feared that the huntsmen as a pair would find a way to counter his plan or hurt his 'bride' if they were left to their own devices for too long. It was *his* magic that had shifted the rock under Elrok's runic inscriptions to throw him past the veil, through it, where he would (should) have been lost for eternity, had the man in the red robe not intervened.

Again, luck was with both of them. Or the fates. Or both.

They would never know which.

They also hadn't quite figured out what to *do* about the problem, despite talking about it for hours with Fanim, Bayetta, and each other. Of all of the different species of elementals, this particular variant was not one often encountered. Neither one of them could think of any time in the last century that one had ever been reported seen (let alone hunted). And when they were, they weren't known to leave survivors.

Stannoth really would have been happier with an elemental of pain. To say that he would have enjoyed a fight with the embodiment of all of the torture in the Abyss instead of trying to battle a force of death itself,

78

well, that was not a fact that set well with anyone else in the warren. (Nor was his remark that a pain elemental would have been easier to walk away from.)

The night had been full of fitful sleep and nightmares for the two of them, and day hadn't given them any fresh ideas. Eventually, it came down to a discussion of what each was capable of and in all honesty, neither of them trusted the other enough to be completely open up until this point.

However, their apparent pending doom was changing their minds a little. Not that anyone could blame them...

"So. Necromancy?"

"Yeap."

"Bit odd, ain't it? Bein' a hunter an' contractin' tae kill, well, monstrous critters? While yer out an' spawnin' 'em fer yerself? Sounds a wee bit like yer huntin' down yer own."

Stannoth shrugged. "Don't do much."

"Killin' monsters or summonin' th' dead?"

"Summoning."

"But... ye do. What kind? Ye able tae pull up th' walkin' dead? Rip a man's bones from 'is body an' make 'em dance? Pull up some demon from th' nightmares o' th' Fallen? Or just tell some rotten bag o' meat tae get out o' th' ground an' clean yer house?"

The dwarf had a way with words. "Spirits. Can't animate."

"Create 'em or call 'em?" he pressed.

Stannoth cast a glance aside to him. "Call. Pull them here. Ones still close. Only fresh. Or angry." He kept staring at him, trying to read his essence to see how the dwarf was taking it. "Control is hard."

"Huh." Elrok looked back at him and shrugged. If he was repulsed, he didn't show it. "Cannae really believe it. I had nae idea that th' Guild had necromancers on staff. They dae know, aye?"

"About me? Yes, they do. A few under contract," the damian answered. "Dark knows dark."

With a snort and a short laugh, the other agreed. "Aye, that old sayin' that evil don't play nicely with other evil. So true, so damned true.Ye ever 'ave one turn on ye?"

"No."

"Yer lucky. I've had tae kill tae many that 'ave before."

"Aye." They walked in silence for another thirty minutes before either one of them spoke up again. The tunnel was getting harder to travel through the further away they got; whatever work Vestalic *should* have been doing, he had failed miserably. If it wasn't for the fact that the Geomancer had seeded the cave with a large vein of those irritating day-glow crystals, Elrok would have been blind.

Stannoth still just wished the the mouth of the world would open up and swallow them all.

"And you?"

"An' me what?"

The taller Huntsman bit back the first thing he thought. "Necromancy. Some deadspeak. Potions. You?"

"Ohhhh. Corpses an' liquid alchemy, eh? Now ain't that a useful combination. Musta been a busy lil' boy down home." Elrok ignored the small smile that passed across the damian's face in an uncharacteristic moment of pride. "Well. I cannae say that I've got all that much better than that."

"What? I should know."

"Aye, aye, I suppose ye should. Alright m'boy. Ye talk tae th' dead. I like tae blow 'em up. I think th' Granalchi call 'em 'manabombs'. I just like tae say it's a bit o' magical boom-boom," he answered with a happy grin.

Stannoth stopped walking and just stared at him. "Magical boom-boom?"

"Aye, that's what I said. What? Ye never call yer stuff anythin' less formal? Or are ye absolutely all business no matter what?"

"Work is work."

"But don't ye ever have any fun with it? Go out, enjoy yerself?"

"We kill things. It isn't fun."

"We're fighters, m'boy. That's what we dae. If ye didn't want tae kill things, then why dae ye dae it?" The dwarf stood there and looked at him, absolutely flabbergasted.

He stood there, and looked down at him for a very long, silent minute. "Because. I have a contract. Important to fulfill."

"Wait, a writ? We all dae. Ye mean just one? Ye work as an assassin fer hire, just fer *one* writ o' execution? Ye get what if ye clear it? A harem? Ye dae. Ye get a harem. I'ma seein' how it is with yer half-blinded ass. Are they made o' gold? Are they *diomisk*? I've heard a great many thins about th' women o' Sycio, an'..."

"No. It's for Zeborak."

Elrok stared right back at him. "An' who's that? Someone that's gone an' pissed off yer mother? Fisked yer sis bent over a barrel?"

You could see the damian's face start to twitch. The dwarf did, and remembered that aura of innocence around him in the veil. Under that innocence... "He did this. To us," he said, slowly pointing to his eyes. "He took it. The sun. He took it. That demon. Bastard son of Belizal. Will find him. Will kill him. Will get it back. For all of us. I *will*."

The conviction in his words sent a chill through the dwarf's bones. Stannoth meant it, meant every word of it, and his voice dripped with more venom than an entire clutch of snakes. In that moment, every nasty little thought the shorter man had for him shriveled up and died. "Ye ain't 'ere fer th' gold or th' glory or even more o' th' gold. Yer doing this fer revenge. An' big revenge, tae... justifiable. Piss, nae even that. It's bloody righteous."

"For my people. We're poor. Can't afford the Guild. Gods don't care. Their servants don't care. Kings don't care. We care. I care. That's why. Isn't fun. Isn't happy. Isn't right. Is what it is. Needs done."

"Surely there's some paladin type or other that'd wannae excise it...?"

"We asked. Order of Light? They said no. Our fault. Our curse. Our problem. They don't care."

"Ye dae know that there's other Orders than just th' ones that toss on th' banner of th' Order o' Light folks, yea? Fisk, th' Order o' Love ain't exactly on friendly terms with 'em. *Serious* fisk, iffin' th' tales are tae be believed, Belizal's th' one that fisked them over an' all that." If Stannoth could have glared, he would have.

"Don't think we tried? They don't care. Heavens don't. The Fallen don't. It's us. *Just* us." He started squeezing his fingers into his palm so hard that the dwarf thought he was going to break something.

He didn't relax them until Elrok reached over and squeezed his fist. "Stanny. Ye'll find 'im. I canna feel it in me heart. Ye will, an' ye won't be alone. I've... I've always had a sense about such. When ye dae, ye just won't be alone."

Unsure of what to make of the dwarf's comments, he slowly nodded his head in thanks. "I will be. Always have been. I stand alone. Always alone."

"Well. We'll have tae see about that. I cannae say that I'ma all tae

81

inclined tae accept that."

Even more confused, the damian took a small step back. "Stop the elemental. First."

"Aye, now that's gonna be a bit o' a problem fer us. I know I said it last night, but... in th' veil, I talked tae a man. Some kinda 'observer,' whatever that's supposed tae mean."

"You said."

"Aye. Well, it's been pickin' at me. Th' bugger saved me, then 'e talked, then 'e sent me back. Talked a blessed lot, tae, I may well add."

The damian was nonplused. "*You* talk a lot."

"Meh. But 'e talked a lot more than I ever dae." Elrok ignored it. "Listen, I saw th' way that Vestalic changed me spellwork. I shouldn't have been able tae step a solid foot back 'ere ever again. So this stranger, observer, whatever, whomever in th' pits 'e is, 'e said somethin' weird."

"Said a lot weird."

"Aye, but this... 'e said 'sand ain't always sand.' Said tae remember it." He forgot, however, that the observer had told him to 'bear witness' to what he did immediately following.

"Say why?"

Elrok shook his head. "Nae, th' prick didn't."

For the fifth time in the last hour, the damian thought on the nature of the creature. "Elemental. It's sand. I saw it. Watched it."

"Aye, sand eternal, th' pale sand o' th' world past th' veil. I dunnae suppose ye have any kinda water magic, dae ye? I mean, if sh's just dirt -"

"Sand," the other corrected.

"- *sand*, then we could wash 'er out? Make 'er melt and drip intae th' seas?"

"No. None."

"Alright. Well. Was worth a bleedin' try. Ye said ye had potions, dunnae have a clue as tae what..."

"Don't carry many."

The short one rubbed his beard and groaned under his breath. "Stilimatharic below us, why didn't ye give yer loyals an' yer devouts a guide on how tae deal with shit like this."

"Gods don't care. He's drunk anyways."

Elrok glanced up and shot him a look. "Ye know, th' observer said that tae me, tae..."

"The drunk-God drinks? You didn't know?"

"That th' patron o' th' Mountains dunnae care. I'm a thinkin' 'e may just be right."

"The damian world view," the other grunted.

His partner scowled as he saw something come down the hallway. "Nae. Just a bit o' a realist." Slowly, the dwarf reached around his back and pulled his hooked swords out of their straps. Instinctively, Stannoth reached back and did the same with his bow. "M'boy? Dae ye think ye can come up with some kinda idea a lil' faster?"

He looked over his shoulder and flashed his teeth in a snarl. There were five of them shambling towards the pair. "Same abominations. Same aura." They weren't in any better shape than the one that was rotting away in its prison in Kepershal. The hulks could walk, and they were able to stand upright, but that was really about it. There was no way to tell if they had just stumbled into the huntsmen or if they had been sent to deal with them.

"Well. They ain't gonna be runin' a race anytime soon. Ye sure we cannae kill 'em?"

"No. Not sure."

"Buuuuut ye don't think we can."

"No. I don't."

Elrok stepped forward and put himself between his partner and the shambling undead. "Fisk. Whelp. Iffin' we cannae kill 'em, best tae make 'em move a wee bit slower. Dunnae think I care tae just walk past 'em an' hope they dunnae come around at a bad time fer us."

"Don't like immortals."

The dwarf gave him a hard chuckle. "Who wants tae live ferever, eh?"

He didn't reply. "They don't."

"True. Very true. An' now me boy, I'm gonna show ye why they make blades. Yer bow ain't exactly all that useful right now, is it?" he taunted with a mirthful smirk. "Ain't like yer gonna make one stop movin' with a shaft o' wood in th' eye."

For a brief moment, Stannoth wondered if the little bastard thought it was all a joke. Maybe it was time to put him well into his place. The look on Elrok's face quickly went from bemusedly cocky to quickly cowed as an arrow all but magically appeared in his bow, nocked and ready to fire.

Without another word, he loosed it into the head of the leading monstrosity in a blur of his hands. Just to prove his point, he landed it dead on in the center of a bloodshot, swollen eye. The impact staggered it, but didn't do much more than that. "Show off," the dwarf grumbled. "But ye didn't stop..."

Then the damian clenched his fist and said a single word. "Burst."

The entire arrow – and the battered hulk's head – disappeared in a flash. *That* knocked it down and barely left even a bloody stump behind. It twitched and tried to find footing on the ground, but it couldn't.

For a change of pace, the short one worked his mouth, but no sounds came out of it.

Stannoth drew, pulled, and fired a second arrow while his partner struggled to express his surprise. Like the first, it impaled the head of the next closest immortal and stuck halfway out the other side. While Elrok expected it to explode again, the damian flexed his fist a second time and said something else.

"Glaciate." That single word turned the arrow to solid ice. The front half of his victim's face did the same thing, and the wretch made an agonized sound deep in its chest. When it reached up to tug the missile out, it did succeed, and the arrow did break free.

Its face followed suit. Elrok started to laugh when it fell to its knees and made another pained gurgling sound from its throat. It might not be dead, but he figured that if they could see the inside of the back of his skull, it wasn't going to stay much of a threat. "I thought ye said ye didn't like th' boom-boom."

"I don't *say* that."

He laughed even harder at that. "Supposin' then it's me turn tae dae some o' th' work."

Stannoth didn't respond. He didn't really need to.

With a speed that belied his bulky stature, the dwarf charged down the hall and eviscerated two of the remaining three wretched souls at once. His swords were truly wicked tools; not much more than a foot and a half long each, the tips were completely bent back to run parallel three inches back against the blade. Three inches that were now coated in viscera.

The attacks pulled his victims down to the ground, but he wasn't done with them yet. While those two writhed in fresh bloody misery, the fifth one attempted to lunge at him with ages-old ruined hands with just two bone-splinters for fingers. Elrok ducked and thrust his swords straight up. It screamed as the hooks tore into its groin and ripped it from crotch to gullet in a single powerful blow.

With all three of his victims a bloody mess on the stone floor, the only thing left to do was keep them from getting back up and walking away. His blades made short work of arms and legs, and he let his partner take the grisly task of gathering the bits up to bury them under chunks of loose stone, off to the side and out of the way.

What they both would have given for the safety to set a fire.

Except... the fight gave Elrok an idea. It dawned slowly, but it dawned. He asked if he had any other special effects with that bow, and the response was perfect. As he explained his idea, it blossomed into a plan, and they liked it. It was completely, totally, and utterly insane, but the two of them agreed that it was probably the best chance that either one of them had to dispose of the beast.

Because, truthfully?

Killing death wasn't something that the sane could do.

As they were being dismembered, all of the wretched bastards that could talk had called out names. Some called out "CHEL!" and "Z'CHEK!". If Stannoth hadn't told Elrok about Lessiana's journals, they wouldn't have realized that those were the names of the wartribes they called home so many lifetimes ago. It was a complicated mess that neither one of them really understood even with the explanation provided by Bayetta *or* the journals.

And, truthfully, neither one of them really wanted to explore the ramifications of what a battle of Divine Will between War and Death presented. It was outside of their pay grade and it was outside of their comfort level. For that matter, it was so far beyond the bounds of rational thought that it gave them both a headache. So, they did the best thing they could.

They ignored it. It was a better question for academics. Or, as the observer hinted, other (holy) idiots.

However, all of the wretches called out a third name. "Sessalaki!"

Now that was more interesting. Nothing in the contract, the journals, or the information that the dwarves eventually provided gave any kind of reference to it. But, since all of them seemed to know it, it was well within the realm of possibility that it was the given name for the elemental (or at least, the name it had given itself).

This, too, was too far outside of their pay grade to question, although they tried to rationalize it anyway. Did she have sentience enough to name herself? If she did, was she something they should try to kill? Should they pass word to the Granalchi? (Assuming, of course, that they weren't already on the way. Two of theirs *were* dead. It wasn't something that the Academy tended to ignore.)

The huntsmen wondered if they should try to capture her, and hand her over to a Temple or an Order somewhere. Or if they could somehow study her. They weren't even sure if they should go back to the warren and try to negotiate with her when she eventually showed her face again. Neither of them really wanted the fight, so was there a chance...?

They thought on it. Then they dropped it. They were being paid to find and kill it.

So, they prepared for just that.

It didn't matter what flavor they were, elementals of any stripe tended to be hard to kill. Mostly they were confined to their home dimension; minions of their own creators, their Gods. They weren't Avatars. They were simply cast in the visage of their creator, just as mortal men and women, but powered by souls so different from humanity and its varied offshoots that it was safest to simply call them 'magic'.

On occasion, they could manifest on their own. Normally though, to make them appear on this plane, you needed a very adept mage, or a Daemon (and a real one at that, not some pit-scraping fear-mongering creature with delusions of grandeur). Yes, you could summon them if you knew the right spell and the right words (in the right language... it's not like they would decide to speak in one of the common tongues of the mortal world).

Controlling them was a different story. Even if you could bring one into this world, there were no guarantees that it would be weak enough to dominate. Sometimes, bigger ones came through by accident. When they did, they were usually pissed.

More than a few abused that power. Since they weren't "mortal," they tended to treat them so poorly that they ran the risk of having them go rogue. Once you realized that your new slave wasn't even one of the races of man start with? It became that much easier to abuse.

That never ended well. It was, sadly, a mistake far too easily made.

When they went rogue, they had to be hunted. On the face of it, it wasn't a unique writ. A difficult one, yes, but not unique. This one, this 'Sessalaki,' she wasn't much different from any other elemental. Single-minded. Driven. Trapped in a world alien to her home.

She was just like every other elemental of any other kind from any other Creator. Inhuman and so far removed from 'rational' thought that they could be understood only by their own kind or by their own God. By and large, many doubted that they were even capable of comprehending their own nature.

So, as they trekked, they thought, and they wondered. What was the nature of death?

Ending life, they determined. Yet, there was more to it than just that. When the end comes, it always comes in a flash. No matter how long someone suffered or how long they lingered, the moment they gave up their souls (or they were taken) comes and goes in a flash. Their demise may be long in coming: they may suffer for minutes, hours, or even years. It is that second, that moment where there is no heartbeat, no breath, no thought; life is gone. No, the nature of death wasn't just what it did, but how.

The nature of death is speed.

Tracking her hadn't been difficult. Between what Elrok saw of her shadow in the ether, and with the blinding fog lifted off of Stannoth's sight, the maze of the outer tunnels wasn't a shield for her any longer. It was where they found her that was interesting: a cavernous room, filled with a handful of twitching bodies impaled on stalagmites or cast into a pool in the middle brimming with things best left to the blissful dreams of necrophiliac zealots and cannibalistic butchers. The elemental floated over it, shifting between a sandy cloud and her dreadful attempt to take a suitable form.

Driven mad, exhausted in confinement, powers muted through centuries of inconceivable effort to reap immortals, Sessalaki still had speed. That speed was both her ally and her enemy in the fight – and it wasn't going to be a fair one.

None of her playthings were in any shape to move about on their own. There was only one that might have been able to – but a pillar of brass and stone had fallen atop it, pinning its legs. Curiously, there were battered dwarven antiques all over the chamber, along with outcroppings of radiant light crystals. Some had been grown into misshapen statues; a kind of poorly-crafted busts of the elemental, likely sad gifts from her demented lover. The room was steeped in history. History, sadly, that nobody had time to entertain the notions of.

With a hiss that sounded much like an hourglass, she pulled herself together and took on a form you could almost mistake for human. She tried her best to make a sword from her right arm as she puzzled her mind around the intrusion of these two insects into her realm.

Even with that much effort expended, she could barely keep her own form. Her left arm continually fell off her shoulder only to be caught by her leg and reabsorbed and remade. Gaping holes in her torso let Elrok see completely through her. Her sand, the very sand itself, was so discolored from decades of disuse that it was barely familiar to the world that had birthed it.

She couldn't craft that sword; she didn't even have the strength for that. It turned into a haggard and frail hooked claw. Neither of them thought it would be sharp enough to slice butter, let alone leather or chain. Looks were deceiving. They weren't sure what she was thinking, although Elrok saw frustration rolling off of her shoulders as easily as Stannoth could (even without a magical aid).

The elemental didn't try to talk or beg for her life. All she did was attack. They thanked every God they worshiped (and a few they didn't) that she was just a pathetic shadow of her former glory. She was strong enough to cause a world of pain, true, but not able enough to kill with just a touch. Stannoth didn't move fast (or far) enough to dodge her when she crossed the cave in half a heartbeat. A cold agony tore through him from stomach to spine when her fingers dug into his armor.

He didn't let go of his bow though. Even as a wave of bile hit the back of his mouth, he took a shot and watched as the arrow flew... and missed her completely. Strangely, when it hit the wall behind her, not only did the arrow detonate (as intended) but the wall cracked (not intended). Then it caved in on itself, and fell to the floor with a crash. A door of solid brass stood there, buried by stone, hidden from everyone on this side of the tunnels.

They didn't have time to realize that they had just found the *other* prize that Aidenchal wanted.

A glowing burgundy ball of mana exploded against her hip as she tried to cut the damian down. The impact sent Stannoth to the floor and forced Sessalaki to literally pull her body back together. The blast disoriented her, and sent her sands flying through the air like a swarm of gnats.

Shuddering in pain, all the archer could do was watch the dwarf fling two more balls of mystical explosives at her, tearing an arm and both of her legs away. They forced her to focus her efforts on him and forget about the sun-blind fool in her hand. The spells were a distraction. Nothing more. She reformed as fast as they hit. That kind of magic wasn't going to be enough to end her on its own.

Her nature would.

Elrok dove out of the way as the elemental unleashed a torrent of raking swipes at him with her hands and feet. Her scream sounded like a hurricane being sucked into a void. It didn't stop until the dwarf's blades gave her true cause to make one (and gave Stannoth another reason to reconsider his thoughts on short blades for a second time in as many hours). His hooksword didn't have to swing very hard to have exceptional results. No, her speed did that for him.

One sword caught her leg. Her momentum made it sheer off cleanly. His other, snagged her ribs. That damn near split her in half. She careened into a side wall; part of her showered the room with a deluge of that awful sand. The rest melded against the cavern as she struggled to reform. "NOW! NOW!" he screamed.

The pain in the archer's gut was immense – but he was the key. If he could have cried, he would have. But he was still the key. So, he couldn't. Her touch had put the fear of the grave into his bones. It wasn't something he'd soon forget. The fear of failing, the fear of missing, the fear of drawing her attention again if she realized what he planned to do...

If her fingers could cause so much pain through his armor, he couldn't imagine the agony if she had touched his skin. He knew she would. Touch him, touch the dwarf, and again, and again. Anything worse than that fleeting instant her hand had ground against his armor, another second of her grip on him, and he would have had dropped his bow. That would have stopped him from taking a second volley at her. The second one was the one that counted.

Elrok did his part. He distracted her. He disrupted her. He bought time, and put her where she could be hurt. He stood there and he screamed at Stannoth. He screamed until his throat was raw. He lobbed another spell at her head, blowing it apart for another instant. She reformed.

She reformed too late.

His arrow didn't need to be perfectly aimed. As shaky as his arm was, it couldn't have been. She wasn't human. She didn't have a 'single' weak spot. No, she was all armor – but conversely, her entire body *was* the weak spot if you had any idea as to what you were doing. If you could figure it out. If they could do it.

And they did.

The arrow hit her just below her throat. It didn't detonate. It didn't freeze. That wasn't its purpose. The tip didn't kill her outright (it couldn't). It didn't even slow her down. She didn't try to comprehend it or puzzle out why they had tried to use something so silly to stop the closest thing to the embodiment of death that either of them would ever see for a very, very, long time.

No, she ignored it, because death is an end – not a journey – and its nature precluded it from learning or growing through experience. The unexpected doesn't matter to death, only the finality of what has been fated. It didn't stop her, so she didn't care. Why should she have? A bit of metal, on a wooden stick? What chaos could it cause a creature born from sand?

You can't kill sand. You can't really cast it to the wind in a cave (not in this stale cavern, at least). There wasn't any water to try and wash her away. But as the man in the red robe had said, sand was not always sand. When they remembered where they had started from, and who it was that worked there...?

...and then remembered what happened to sand if you applied the right type of heat?

They had more in common with the Glassworkers than either one of them had thought. "SEAR!"

A second, a third, and a fourth arrow lanced into her. They burned white hot and fused each grain of sand together. Sessalaki twisted and turned; her body melted into an unrecognizable molten lump. Her face was the final thing to go, and her terrible beauty dissolved into a spreading pool of pale gold, liquid glass and slag. It wasn't enough, it couldn't be enough, to leave her like that.

A final arrow of ice was shot into her ruined shell. The enchanted missile froze what was left of her, and just as simple as that, he gave the

90

nearly-immortal blonde a true heart of glass. Stannoth gave his partner a weak nod, and the dwarf took care of the rest. One last ball of Elrok's magic struck her dead center and sent glass shards flying everywhere.

The man with the metal faceplate sagged back against the cave wall and wrapped his arms around his midriff. Destroyed or not, the elemental's touch still radiated through him. She had put a lot of energy into trying to kill him; maybe she had realized that he was that dangerous, or maybe she just didn't know how to channel her own power anymore. He lifted his armor up and went a few shades paler when he saw the damage left behind in her wake.

She had put so much effort into destroying him that even his chainmail had turned black where she had touched it. The skin below it had turned a pale gray, with blisters below every place where the metal had been corrupted and had easily burned through the leather padding under it. The dwarf felt his throat go painfully dry when he realized how much pain his ally had to be in, and opted to let one of his last secrets come into play.

Elrok knelt down next to him and pushed his hands aside. As the damian watched, a soft nimbus of light started to radiate from his hands. The touch was soothing. A broken rib started to stitch itself back together while a burn went lukewarm, then comfortably cool. He didn't even notice a change in the dwarf's aura while he worked. "Healer?"

"Ye've had yer secrets with yer magic, I've had a few o' mine." He looked over at the pile of broken glass on the rough floor and embedded into the walls. "Think th' bitch is gone fer good, or did we just buy us some time?"

Stannoth looked long and hard at the remains before finally answering. "Gone."

His companion let out a long, almost whistling sigh of relief. "Well. That's surely a different way tae earn me pay fer this bugger o' a fight. Dunnae think I'd want tae put up with a second round with th' damned thin'."

As the pain melted into a tolerable throb, the archer looked over at the uncovered brass door. There was something massively wrong with the energy around it. *Massively.* The longer he stared the more he realized that something was shielding it from his view. A few minutes later, he noticed something else. The door wasn't simply enchanted.

It was smoking.

There wasn't much. It was acrid... and smelled of burning flesh. That didn't bode well.

He struggled to his feet, ignoring the protests from his diminutive companion. Then something started to *pound* on the door, and even the dwarf had to pay attention to that. Neither one of them wanted a fresh fight, but by the looks of things, they weren't going to have a choice as to if they wanted one or not.

They really didn't.

The pair approached it nervously, completely in the dark about where it led and, and what was going on behind it. They should have paid more attention to what was going on behind *them*. A small drift of sand, scattered from Elrok's spells, started to coalesce over the shattered creature. Glass shards started to spin up off the ground, once more trying to form the vanquished elemental for a futile heartbeat before a blast of fire into their center tore what little life the agent of Death had left completely away. The shards fell to the ground with an ominous crash and gave them all too brief notice of the newest arrival

Whipping around at the sound, they were greeted by someone they didn't expect at all. Clad in armor of leather and chain exactly like theirs, with a cloak almost exactly like Stannoth's, Bayetta stood there with a smile. "Well then. 'ello boys," she said – with an odd, almost purring inflection to her voice.

"Bay? What are ye...?"

"Checkin' tae make sure that I'd not have tae drag another pair o' bodies out. Thank ye fer nae droppin' dead." she answered. "Ye got 'er done. Damned impressed I am, with th' both o' ye."

Stannoth pointed at the door with his bow. "No time. Problem."

Her face blossomed into a massive smile. "Aye, 'tis. But it ain't yers."

"Fight? Smoke? Could be anything. Can't see," he argued.

The little dwarf nodded, the smile never leaving her lips. "Aye. Ye can't. Ye cannae see out, *they* cannae see in. 'Tis workin' more or less exactly how it should an' all. Dammit though, that gate just shouldn't be uncovered. I suppose I'ma gonna have tae dae somethin' about it."

"I think what th' boy means is that there's obviously somethin' goin' on past that damned door dearie, somethin' that may well spill over intae th' warren. Th' smoke alone, there's somethin' that ain't right about it..."

Bayetta raised her hand to quiet them. It didn't hurt that the hand had a very large bag that jingled just like gold dangling from it. "What's goin' on past there is a reckonin'. One that needs tae happen, an' one that dunna need ye, either of ye, tae be involved. Ain't th' job fer any o' us, nae ye, nae me. Ye were right. That elemental? It ain't exactly th' real goal. Just a problem fer us bein' in th' way."

"You're a hunter?" Stannoth grunted. It was much more of a statement than a question.

"Aye. I am. Th' Master sent me 'ere tae make sure that th' door there ain't get disturbed 'till all's ready fer it tae be opened. I sent fer ye tae make sure that when th' time was right, we'd not have tae worry about what was takin' apart th' folk down 'ere. Ye both did damn well, damn well altogether; damn well *together*."

"Fanim know? Vestalic?" the damian growled. He was starting to share Elrok's post-veil disgust over being used by the short fiskers. It replaced the other disgust he had for just working with them.

"Nae Fanim ain't have an idea in that sad lil' head o' 'is, except fer bein' obsessed with th' thought o' old orcs runnin' roughshod through th' tunnels. Th' funny thin' though, is th' Gemwarden wasn't all that wrong at all. There *is* an orc, more than one, an' they've been doin' nae small amount o' damage. Just... up there," she explained. "An' Vestalic is a mad dog without a bone. Didn't know a damned thin' about any damned thin'."

"Open the door," Stannoth pressed. "Orcs die well."

Bayetta shook her head. "Nae, ye won't. I won't. Not this time. Sorry tae ruin yer rampage, but, yer just about done with yer contract. One more thin' tae dae, then, I've got somethin' fer ye..."

"Oh? An' what is it?" the other dwarf finally asked. "Ye've been lyin' tae us th' entire time we've been down 'ere, and I canae say that I'm exactly happy an' all about it."

She pulled another coinpurse from inside the leather cloak she was wearing and showed it to both of them. "One hundred an' fifty coins o' gold fer yer pay, each. An' I'll be doublin' it iffin' ye dae one last thin' fer me."

"Terms?" the taller of the trio asked.

The pair looked at each other for a few seconds before turning back to her. "An' what'd that be, oh dear daughter o' a lovely lady? I cannae say sh' is gonna be all that happy tae hear about any o' this th' next time

93

I'ma off on me own an' spendin' time back home."

"Oh, but this one is a tad easy. An' then ye won't have tae worry about this place ever again."

"Terms?" the damian grunted (again).

The Guild representative tossed them both their individual bags. "Ye dunna tell a damn soul about what ye've seen, where this tunnel leads tae, th' door right thereabouts, an' sure as all that there be sufferin' down in th' pits, *ye dae nae say a damned word about what ye think yer hearin' from behind it,*" she answered. "Double yer pay, and fer that matter, ye can take whatever bits o' this damned bitch 'ere back with ye that ye'd want tae."

"I cannae see how broken glass could be worth a worm's spit," Elrok muttered, a little shocked by this turn of events (and focused on the wrong part of her offer).

She sighed. "Well, I cannae say I'm tae surprised ye can't, but th' archer can. Glass arrowheads distilled by th' essence o' death? Quite bleedin' surprised 'e ain't tryin' tae make a bag outta 'is cloak tae shove 'er intae it yet."

"What about the immortals?"

That made her pause. "What about 'em?"

"Still a danger."

"Cannae say I'll be sleepin' tae well knowin' th' poor sods are rottin,' sufferin,' an' lost tae th' dark..."

"They'll rot in th' Abyss, tae...," Bayetta practically whined.

Stannoth didn't accept that. "You can't judge fate. They deserve an end."

"Vestalic doesn't," she openly whined.

"That boy wasn't trapped in 'er bed; 'e came intae it an' just simply chose tae act on 'er madness," Elrok groused as he poked at Sessalaki's shards. "Th' boy 'as a point tae 'im. Ye've got pull with th' Company, an' th' Company has resources that ain't either o' us has got now nae ever will."

"So dae kings an' queens. Yer point?"

"Your word. Help lift their curse?"

"Ye'll get our words in return that ain't nae a part o' this ever happened, not 'ere, not elsewhere."

Bayetta was less than thrilled by their terms, but... they had a point, and she had to admit it. "Aye. Dunnae know what ye think *I* canna dae about it, but, aye, I'll pledge tae 'elp 'em find some form or other of peace o' death."

"And," Stannoth gave her an expressionless stare. "Double pay. This never happened."

"Aye. Double pay, this never happened, an' I'll be makin' sure that th' Guild knows ye both did all yer contract tasked ye with. Nothin' less. An'! I'll tell th' Gemwarden that th' cave fell in 'ere. Nae worries about anyone findin' th' door, so ye can rest yer minds that I'll find a way tae say ye be abusin' th' deal."

"One other thin'," Elrok added.

The woman sighed at him. "An' what else ye makin' demands from me on? About bloody actin' like it's kinda extortion."

"No idea what," Stannoth interjected. "Not this time."

"Well. I damn well dae. I ain't gonna budge on this one, nae, ain't nae bloody way. Our people, our kin. They ain't in th' veil. They've been cast past it. There's critters there, nasty as all pits critters, an'... they need tae come home."

"Past it? Ye think there's a one o' us that has th' power tae get intae that? Even iffin' we wanted tae?"

"We dunnae, *dunnae* leave our people behind. Nae there, nae there o' all places. Yer word − ye'll be callin' fer priests, ye'll be callin' fer mages. They get relief o' some kinda or other. I'll be back tae check, tae, an' iffin' they ain't gone an' safe..."

"Fer th' sake o' all that's right in th' world... aye aye, I will make sure that there's a way made tae get 'em either back 'ere as spirits tae be a part o' th' land, or moved on tae their next life. An' nae a damned word about th' door, or ye'll be dealin' with problems a tad bit o' worse than just a sad lil' elemental."

They looked at each other again. They managed to say a lot without saying a word, and that smile never left Bayetta's face. After a few long (and awkward) moments later, they agreed to do the only thing they really could. "What door?" Elrok deadpanned.

They decided that this never happened.

It had been a job in a *complicated* pursuit of coin − no matter what Elanis had said.

V. THE BLINDSIDED

Talonbur was asleep in his bed when someone lit the lamp beside it. The young blonde whore next to him took one look at the intruder through bleary, drunken eyes and did the only thing she could: she scampered out of the room as quick as her wobbly legs would let her. He didn't, however. In fact, he didn't even move. Too much wine and too many overpriced wenches.

He apparently wasn't grieving too much over his wife.

It wouldn't have mattered even if he was.

He didn't even know that his health had been in jeopardy from the moment he stepped into her office. For a man who prided himself on knowing the affairs of his house, he failed to consider that there could be a cost for his tone. He surely did not expect that word would reach Lady Elanis that he had threatened her hunters at the Vault. He just didn't have any idea at all.

What he ended up having, however, was a writ. It was a quick death with a knife in his heart deep enough to nail him into the mattress. A hand covered his mouth to keep him from screaming; she left the blade in and twisted it to make sure he learned something... just for good measure. A short lesson, true, but, still a lesson.

On the chance that he could somehow still hear her, the Matriarch of the Southern Guild bent down and whispered in his ear. "My boys are mine, and mine alone, to take to task. That's only when, or if, they deserve so. Did you forget that warning at my office? Hm? You thought that threatening their lives would be forgotten? No. Forgiven? No. Not

96

in this life. Not in the next. *Not* by me."

She left without bothering to listen for a reply.

Fanim hadn't been wrong about everything. There *was* an orc in the tunnels. It was dead – risen and defiled, ruined in the grave. It was hard to say why it was here (a secret guarded behind a door that they swore didn't exist), but like the other questions in the last few days, why and how weren't their concern. However, Bayetta had seen it on her way to check on their progress – and a couple more gold to dispose of the beast was still a couple of extra pieces of gold.

It looked like the orc had tried to use magic to summon and bind souls of long dead animals. That probably meant it had been some kind of land-mage in life... probably a shaman, given the tribal, nomadic nature of any of the orcish empires. All it had actually succeeded in doing was to make a few mindless shades that paced back and forth in front of it. Sometimes they lunged at it, ineffectually trying to bite at him. Sad and futile attempt to fill an insatiable hunger on their part; it was impossible to guess why the orc had tried to call them to begin with.

The hunters were quick about it. Stannoth easily wrested one of his spirits away – some kind of translucent and decrepit goat – and used it to harass the befouled tusker. The dwarf moved in to work right after. He plowed his way through with small bursts of magic that effortlessly dispersed the remaining six shades, one after another, making them vanish back to wherever they had been called from.

By the time the shaman recovered from the attack from its stolen minion, Elrok had swung his hooksword and eviscerated it. Rancid clumps of black mold and soil spilled free from its skin. With a pained groan, it futilely attempted to force him away. It didn't work; Elrok was one step ahead of it. More accurately, he was one step behind it. Before he finished turning, his blades had cut the tendons from the back of the orc's knees and drove it to the rough floor. When it fell, he used the hooks to catch its shoulders and wrenched the beast upright to face the archer.

"So. Where tae after this?"

Stannoth gave a silent shrug and pulled back on his bow. "Closest Guild office. Dawnfire."

"Nae desire tae see Civa, eh?"

"Civan winters get cold. Dawnfire – coastline. Warm coastline."

"Jungles an' beaches an' all that, eh?"

"Yes."

The damian mulled over his reasoning and looked down at his companion. "Their army is weak. Could be extra work."

Elrok pondered that for a moment. "Oh! Aye. That ugly crusade business. What in th' pits made 'em think tae launch a war intae th' deserts o' Sycio? I ain't exactly risk averse an' all, but... damn. Dae ye have any idea th' kindae stuff that got found in that cesspit?"

"Gods were with them. So they said."

"Pft. That red-robed man knew what 'e said when 'e said th' Gods dunnae care. Ye know... I heard, an' I swear this is true, that th' only reason that th' Dawnies were able tae even hold ontae th' port city there was because some blonde lil' girl pulled their collective asses outtae th' fire. An' nae just once, but twice."

Stannoth sighted his bow and shook his head. "Right. Not likely."

"Eh. With th' holy fiskers they sent tae that place? Gave th' entirety o' the campaign tae th' Order o' Love at th' start? Absolutely anythin' canna be possible." He shrugged. "But. Nae important."

"We have seen stranger."

"Aye, now if that ain't th' truth." He looked over at the archer and tugged the orc back just a hair more. "Dawnfire, ye said?" "Yes."

After a few moments of quiet while he leisurely aimed the bow at the orc, Elrok stole a glance at his partner. "Walkin' alone, standin' alone?"

He thought about it for a minute and let the faintest excuse of a smile flit over his lips. "Hope not."

"Aye. Kinda hopin' not either," the dwarf answered, with a look to match. "Still don't like ye."

"Or I you."

"Good. Then we're gonna be workin' together an' all?"

The bow made a soft 'twang' as the arrow was loosed. The orc's head whipped backwards, the magic holding him together expiring on impact. "Yes."

A pair of cold black eyes looked down at them from a crack in an alcove over their heads. The exchange was music to what passed for the reaver's ears.

The *'observer'* in the red robe? He would have been *utterly* disappointed if they hadn't left together. His newly-conscripted watcher didn't want to consider how dangerous the Man of the Red Death would be if he had been made... *utterly* disappointed.

There was just one last thing: Elanis wasn't the only woman with old business still to resolve.

A few weeks later, the Geomancer was not resting peacefully. The dwarves had decided that just trying to find ways to end his supposed immortality was simply too good for him. It was difficult to come up with a place to put a man who could twist the very ground around him to meet his every need in order to keep him from getting away... but it wasn't impossible.

They first secured his hands and feet with chains anchored into the floor and ceiling of the pit the maddened immortal and been stored in (and eventually buried under – Bayetta's promise unfulfilled; a problem to be resolved... someday). Then they flooded the pit. Plans were already underway to build a shrine to the victims over it. It was a unique punishment. He would drown every second of every day until his magic faded or the cave collapsed in on him. His kin wouldn't even have to hear him scream. Men and women and children would come to the shrine every day, pay their respects, and honor the dead while he agonized beneath their feet.

It was a perfect solution for everyone but him.

Almost.

Not much more than a month went by before Vestalic had a visitor. The locals had no idea she was there, or that she had managed to work out a way to boil away most of the water in the pit. They didn't know she had been digging around in their homes before either – but she wouldn't have been doing her job if they did. Vestalic dangled there, blistered and burned, every inch of him flaming red, steam coursing out of his every pore.

It made for a good start to her task. "I don't like having to come back to a job," she sighed. "I cut your throat, you stay dead. That's how it should be. That's how it's supposed to work. But, did you? Did you? No. Not only did you not *stay* dead, you kept doing things that my boss didn't like. You know that, don't you?

"I've never had to hunt a dead thing before. Not sure if I like it or not just yet. I do like what he paid me. But I don't like that I had to give it back until I finished this. You're the first thing I've never been able to kill, do you know that? Never been a problem before. No, not ever a problem at all."

She jumped down into the pit and gave a satisfied little sigh as the quickly-cooling water put a tingle places she didn't mind having one. Midnight-blue hair floated in the water behind her as she pulled a trio of claws off of her hip and began to fasten them, one by one, on the top of her right wrist. She wore a deceptively thin silken red dress that contrasted nicely with the pair of black bracers on her forearms.

You wouldn't think she was dressed for a fight.

It made her job so much easier if that's exactly what you thought.

"You've made all kinds of problems. Little tiny fish swimming in the wrong kind of pond. You jumped into a big sea of things, you know that, right? He's got his hands in the Midlands. He's got his hands right in the middle of all of the nationalism sweeping through the Civans. The arms trade to the Dawnfire folk has been absolutely amazing! They are playing perfectly off of each other and nobody – not the Kingdoms, not the Empires, not the League, not the Hunter's Guild, not the Granalchi, not the Orders of Light, not the varied Daemons of the Abyss, nobody! - has any idea that he's playing everyone.

"Do you understand that? He is everywhere these tunnels can take you, and he's everywhere the sun hits from continent to continent. He is where water is wet and shadows are dark. Then along comes *you,* a little upstart pissant of a *dwarf* and you start making a mess *right under him*! Quite literally, *right under his feet!*

"Now, I don't get paid," she sighed, "until you're dealt with."

Vestalic couldn't talk. He just hung there and... twitched. She started to run her claws across the gaping wound in his throat, examining her original handiwork. "Suppose I'm lucky to be getting paid at all. He doesn't take failure well. He whipped one of his girls instead of me for not only for *your* failure to die, but also for *your* audacity to continue *your* rampages. He made me watch! That was bad enough. It was nothing short of absolutely grueling and I didn't enjoy it one bit.

100

"Well, neither did the girl. Poor thing could barely stand by the time he was done. You and I are both lucky he decided to work his temper out on that poor slave, because you? *You* would *not* like me half as much right now if he had taken that out on *me*. Bad enough he made me *watch*. Did I *mention* it wasn't fun? It *wasn't*. I ended up with some of her on me. Took me the rest of the day to get her scrubbed off of this gown!

"I, personally, would be just as happy to leave you here like this. He's not me. He wants your head. Specifically, your head. Not the rest of you. Just that. What's going to be fun about that is that neither one of us are confident that taking your head is actually going to kill you. I think that offends him somehow. You know those Death-worshipers, don't you? They don't take kindly to things that don't die. You should know that better than anyone; since you are one, after all.

"Well. You were one. Not sure how you feel about taking up that particular line of worship now. Either way. If this doesn't kill you, you'll have plenty of time to wish it did. We're not so sure how much it's going to sting, either. I'm betting on a lot. We're not sure if you'll feel the pain afterward, either, or even if you will still be able to feel the rest of your body floating down here when it's all done.

"However! There is some good news. I've had to talk, at length, with representatives of other warrens over the last few months. Not just about this mess. Lots of various reasons. So help me, if I have to hear your absolutely Gods-*awful* and *appalling* dialect that manages to mangle everything that is good about the spoken word at any point in the next few years? I'm going to go crazier than you are.

"I thank every Godling that will ever look down upon us with scorn from that puffed up place they call the Mount or any of the fallen that look up from the pit with delight and envy that I am not responsible for transcribing your misbegotten language on paper. I would curse myself every minute of every day to do it and frankly? I imagine it would make me go bald.

"The good news? I don't have to do it anymore! The second your head hits the water? I made him promise that I don't have to listen to any more of you diminutive, irritating, and utterly pathetic wretches. Not for a long, long time. I'm hoping you can be happy with me over that. I am absolutely delighted.

"He told me to do something else, too, just to be sure. It's simple,

101

really. You and that creature you were playing with have cost him a *lot* of gold. He paid for Granalchi transportation for both sets of hunters. He paid for the wizards you killed. He had to pay to get a message to the Darkfather. He had to buy out the contract of the second damian to get him transferred out here. He had to pay for *me*. Oh, and despite the opinions of his concubines, I am *not* some cheap whore. You do understand that you have cost him a *lot* of gold, don't you?"

"Aidenchal does *not* like to lose a *lot* of gold."

She traced around the edges of the gash in his neck. She moved slowly. Very, very slowly. Vestalic tried to scream – but the rocks that his jailers had sewn into his mouth to keep him from doing just that were doing their job. "It's so simple," she said as she poked and prodded at the wound. He said to just, oh... how was it? Oh yes. 'Make it hurt. Take your time, girl. Just make it *hurt*.' I can do that."

"Just so you know. *My* name -- in case you *can* ever talk again and want one to curse? My name is Karistina Semtune. He calls me his little Lady Claw." She smiled wide at him.

"I like it. Don't you?" Her claws glistened in the dark. And then she went to work.

End: Saga of the Dead Men Walking
Blindsided

102

COMPENDIUM OF THE DAMNED, DIVINE, AND ALL THINGS IN-BETWEEN

Age of Misfortune
*The Age of Misfortune covers a period of Kora's history where several...
less than pleasant... events happened in a relatively short period
(roughly twenty to thirty years) of time. Most of these events can be
traced back to one person that Stannoth and Elrok will eventually meet,
even though they've already come close to him by the end of their first
adventure together.*

Agromah
*A fallen continental-kingdom to the North of Civa, Dawnfire, and more,
across the Nightmare Sea. It is believed by most that the armies of the
Order of Love abandoned the Order of Flames in the face of a demonic
army lead by Archduke Belizal and his son, Zeborak. It's this belief (false
as it is) that lead to Niasmis being exiled from the Upper Pantheon, and
her followers to suffer the Hardening.*

Archduke Belizal
*A true Daemon of horrific power, not only is he responsible for the
destruction of Agromah, his son holds the curse that has stolen the sun
from the Damian peoples.*

Blackstone Trading Company (The BeaST)
*The largest trading company in the entire western hemisphere, the
BeaST is owned and run by Master Aidenchal, a dedicated follower of
Uoom, and it has holdings that stretch from Civa to Mathiea and*

everywhere – literally everywhere – else.

Candle-Crystal
A small crystal that grows in the undertunnels near and below the Midland Wastes, primarily near the Kepershal Gem Warrens. If they were ever to be mined out of the tunnels and sold on the open market, someone – someone like Master Aidenchal – would stand to make enough profit to buy a Kingdom, if he so wished.
He wishes.

Chel
One of the two ever-warring tribes in the Midland Wastes. Cursed (blessed?) years ago by the God of War to have everlasting life as long as they continued to battle the Z'Chek, they have a unique relationship with the God of Death. Mainly, they are a thorn in His side, and it is rumored some of His reapers nearly went mad trying to collect on what is rightfully His.

(The) Crusades
A massive war launched by the Kingdom of Dawnfire against the Dunesires of Sycio. The conflict spanned years, and at a great cost of life for everyone involved.

Crystal Kingdoms
The combined Kingdoms of the Dwarven people, with each major underground city referred to as part of the Gemset. The Kingdoms are ruled by the Underlord and his sons, the Underprinces. Except for one, who likes to beat things up more than he does rule. Go figure – a dwarf that prefers brawling to diplomacy.

Damian
Mostly human in appearance (albeit taller than the average, and pale-skinned), Damians are an odd race. Thought to have come about through the mating of humans and elves centuries ago, they were ostracized and shunned by both the Kingdoms of Men and the Elven Kingdoms. Still, that didn't stop humans or elves from siring more of them any time the chance for such... exciting... endeavors came about. When their leaders made a pact with the son of Archduke Belizal hundreds of years back, the demon turned on them and cursed their race: any that saw the sun would die. Forced underground, they figured out a way to counter the curse, but... not without some difficulty.

Darkfather
The lord and ruler of the Damian people.

Dwarves
Short, stocky, blunt, and they have a nearly universal tendency to drink first and brawl drunkenly. They are the (usually) undisputed masters of everything below the surface. They talk to the stone and the stones talk back, which means one of two things – either they have a connection to the world that nobody else can match, or generations of drinking has caused severe mental deficiencies and liver damage. It really depends on who you ask. Disliked by most, and in the occasional war against some of the other races that call the underground their homes, you cannot discount their abilities with geomancy (even if their language is such a bastardized form of Common that it makes your head hurt to transcribe into written word).

Deadspeak
The language of the dead. Exceedingly difficult to master, it's practiced (sometimes perfectly, sometimes poorly) by necromancers the world over. Learn to speak it, and you can begin to learn the secrets of what's beyond the veil. Don't learn to speak it, and you save yourself inevitable psychosis and madness.

Defiled
The 'defiled' are mortal/natural creatures that have been exposed to or twisted by Abyssian magic/auras to the point that they have become monsters in their own right. Corpses that have arisen from the dead on their own volition are lumped into this category, as are animals (or even people) that have been corrupted past the point of the Laws of Normality. Creatures, and even inanimate objects, that have been turned pose as much of a threat to the living world as demons... and some demons have been been known to start out this way.

Drakeforged/Astan's Irregulars
Two mercenary companies that call Goldenglass home. They don't do much work outside of Mathiea, but they've done some work in Sycio as a result of the Crusades.

Deepshadows
There are things under the surface that aren't made of rock, things that the dwarves cannot touch, and wouldn't even if they could. Things that are odd, things that are ancient, things that are powerful, and things

that live in the darkest of tunnels in the deepest of caves, things that whisper stories and thoughts and offers of power through every crack, every tiny little shaft. These things live in the Deepshadows; a place that no light will ever touch.

Elementals
They are, to their home planes of origin, what humans are to Kora. Creatures born and bred by the direct hand of their Gods, they are as alien to humanity as demons and angels. That doesn't stop people from trying to control them, of course, but... people are stupid.

(The) Family
In Damian culture, the Family oversees the dead. It is considered a great honor to be one, and every Damian that dies is to come under their hands to prepare them for the afterlife.

Gemwarrens
Cities and outposts of the Crystal Kingdoms, and are managed by Gemwardens.

Geomancer
Mages that can control dirt, rocks, crystals, more dirt, and so on.

Golden Empire of Mathiea
One of the four great Kingdoms and Empires of the Western World, the Golden Empire of Mathiea is far to the south of the Kingdom of Dawnfire, and east of Sycio. They are a continental-Empire, with only two small regions that aren't fully in their control on the far eastern side of their territory. They have a simple rule: don't act against us, and we won't act against you. It tends to work out very well for them.

Goldenglass
One of the larger cities in Mathiea, it's also one of the most impenetrable. Don't fall in the water. Drinking it isn't always the most advisable option either, unless you really trust the person that's serving you a cup.

Granalchi
Masters of the arcane. They bow to no God as a whole, but simply seek to control and use elemental magic in any and all forms. While commune with the Gods to access upper and lower planes of magic is frowned upon, it is not verbosely forbidden by the Headmasters of the

Academy. That being said, anyone that seeks to explore the vast power held in the Abyss is **strongly** encouraged to do so off of campus grounds. They'll also deny any knowledge of any student caught using forbidden arts – not that they aggressively seek to punish anyone that does.

Hunter's Guild
The Hunter's Guild is an organization filled to the brim with mercenaries, assassins, battlemages, and anyone else willing to make a quick bag of coin hunting people or things down. They get paid handsomely for their efforts, and the payments get bigger the more dangerous or morally questionable the contract is. They aren't to be confused with the more 'noble' exorcists and paladins, but they can do a wonderful job cleaning up any mess that the priestly Orders leave behind.

Kepershal Gemwarrens
Neither one of the largest nor one of the most important of the Gemwarrens, nevertheless, Kepershal was a stalwart outpost of Dwarven military might during the last Underwar.

Lady Elanis
Guildmatron of the Southern Hunter's Guild. She doesn't just call the shots; she has an innate ability to assess a situation and determine who or what needs to die when and where and usually how. Sweet and kind on the outside, she's a cold-hearted calculating monster in her heart. Rumor is she can make Writs of Execution appear out of thin air (and it's hard to call it a rumor when it's actually true).

Makaral
The Berzerker God, the God of War.

Master Aidenchal
The man with the money. The richest individual in the world that doesn't own a Kingdom or Empire with a border, his holdings are as vast as the eye can see.

(The) Midlands
An ugly, barely hospitable chunk of land in the middle of the Equalin Mountains, it's home to various nomads and wartribes. At best they're uncultured shepherds and growling brutes, at worst, the wartribes are as barbaric as you can get. Still, some of the tribes on the distant edges aren't THAT bad... although there is a matter of an unceasing, eternal war being waged between the God of War and the God of Death right in

the middle of it that leads to the perception that they're all violent brutal barbaric hordes. That's not necessarily the wrong idea, but it is the perception.

Niasmis
Banished from Her rightful place next to the top of the Mount of Heaven by the other Gods and Goddess for an infraction against the Goddess of Flame that She truthfully is not guilty of, the Goddess of Love is considered by nearly everyone to be the least of the Divine, and as such, holds power only in the lowest regions of the Heavens, and... well...
...She has a bit of a chip on Her shoulder because of it...

Nightshade
War-forged necromancers in service to the Darkfather. There aren't many of them, and for the sake of every other Kingdom and Empire, that's probably a good thing.

Orathium / Orcs
The Orathium Empire used to be one of the most powerful in the world. Used to be. When their eyes and their methods pushed against the Kingdoms of Men one too many times, they were targeted for one of the largest acts of genocide in history (second only to the fall of the Elven Kingdoms). When they attempted to take refugee underground by way of brute force, the dwarves and damians treated them to a second round of punishment. Not many are left, and those that are, are in hiding.

Reavers
Disgusting monsters that hide in the Veil. They don't cross over to the mortal realms, but woe unto any soul that manages to cross over without landing on the edge of the Heavens or the Precipice of the Abyss.

Shadewells
Souls of fallen damians reside here, or at least, so it's thought. Few but the Darkfather and the Family can hear their voices in the deep and in the dark.

Stilimatharic, the Stonehewn
The God of Dwarves, Orcs, Goblins, Trolls, and other things that wander the tunnels and caverns below the surface. Also known as the Drunk God — because let's be honest, nobody sober would have created the

dwarves. He is not the God of the Damians, however, and they openly view Him with scorn.

Sycio
Complicated. In short, the deserts of Sycio were once ruled by the Dunesires and Duneprinces. As a culture, they had no problems consorting with the dead, the damned, and even had a strong workforce of corpses – a good body is a shame to waste. During the Age of Misfortune, one of those demonic alliances resulted in... why don't we say "aggressive discomfort" ...felt across all of the land. They earned the distinction of being targeted by most of the western kingdoms to... correct... the error of their ways in the vast Crusades that waged for years at the behest of the Queen of Dawnfire and the express desire of her Holy General, Johasta Fire-Eyes.

(The) Underwar(s)
The Dwarven Kingdoms and the Damians used to get along. Then they didn't. Neither of them liked the incursions by the Orcs or the Goblins either, and... things happened. The Damians and Dwarves fought to a stalemate while the Orcs were escorted by force out of the underground and the goblins chased far away from either of the surviving kingdoms.

Uoom
The God of Death. Uoom's Ledger is the only record in all of creation of every man, woman, child, animal, angel and demon that was ever born or made – coupled with an ever-growing list of souls that have been and will be sent to everlasting eternity in one form or another.

Z'Chek
One of the two major wartibes of the Midlands, they are locked in a constant battle with the Chel, by instruction of Makaral, the God of War.

Zeborak
Son of Archduke Belizal, this Daemon is sadistic in ways that defy imagination. One of his greatest accomplishments was cursing the Damian race to die whenever they would see the sun. He is actively hunted by an entire race of people, and his whereabouts are, at current, unknown (though incorrectly believed to be beside his father, ruling somewhere deep in the Abyss).

ABOUT THE AUTHOR

Hailing from the Parkersburg area in West Virginia, USA, Joshua is the son of the wonderful woman that illustrated the cover artwork (hi mom!) and a stay at home adoptive father to his five furry demonic overlords, or as other people call them, cats. A geek, a gamer, and a cosplayer for charity, he's spent far too much time thinking about geopolitics and societal norms, so trying his hand at being a writer seemed like a good idea... it's less scary than the real world.

Usually.

OH! And be sure to check out the other books and short stories set in this universe!

Saga of the Dead Men Walking: Snowflakes in Summer
&
Saga of the Dead Men Walking: Fearmonger

Snowflakes takes place long before the events in this one, and Fearmonger well after Blindsided... but... Joshua will get caught up. He's a fiction writer. You can trust him.

www.ingramcontent.com/pod-product-compliance
Lightning Source LLC
Chambersburg PA
CBHW020621120726
47905CB00003B/890